Clemency Pogue:

The HOBGOBLIN PROXY

JT Petty

Illustrated by Will Davis

Simon & Schuster Books for Young Readers
New York London Toronto Sydney

SIMON & SCHUSTER BOOKS FOR YOUNG READERS
An imprint of Simon & Schuster Children's Publishing Division
1230 Avenue of the Americas, New York, New York 10020

SIMON & SCHUSTER BOOKS FOR YOUNG READERS is a trademark of
Simon & Schuster, Inc.
Book design by Einav Aviram
The text for this book is set in Cochin.
The illustrations for this book are rendered in graphite.
Manufactured in the United States of America
10 9 8 7 6 5 4 3 2 1
Library of Congress Cataloging-in-Publication Data
Petty, JT (John T.)
Clemency Pogue : the hobgoblin proxy / J.T. Petty.— 1st ed.
p. cm.
Sequel to: Clemency Pogue, fairy killer.
Summary: Clemency Pogue and the hobgoblin Chaphesmeeso begin a
quest to rescue lost fairies, find a boy-goblin's changeling, and restore
equilibrium to the Make-Believe.
ISBN-13: 978-1-4169-0768-8
ISBN-10: 1-4169-0768-8
[1. Fairy tales. 2. Goblins—Fiction. 3. Fairies—Fiction.] I. Title.
PZ8.P45Clg 2006
[Fic]—dc22
2005022455

FOR MOM AND ROSY

FOR BECKY!
FOR SAMANTHA!
FOR CRYING OUT LOUD!

PROLOGUE

ALL CHILDREN GROW, but not always up, and not always older.

Gilbert Mess grew big before he grew up. He was quicker and larger than any of his classmates, stronger even than some of his teachers; the only thing that topped him was a confusion of red hair eerily similar to the cross-hatching of the red rubber ball in his hands. Gilbert had been elected captain of one of the day's kick-ball teams. As he chose his players, Gilbert's eyes kept reluctantly returning to his little brother, Inky.

"Martha . . . Reed . . . Laura . . . Kyle . . . Kathryn . . . David . . . I'll take . . . what's-his-name, the kid with one leg. . . ." The names were called, and kick-ball players ran (or hopped) to join their sides, leaving Inky closer and closer to being all alone.

Inky had a head shaped like a chestnut and the look of a frog prince about him—a confidence that his days being tiny and slimy were few. It was a confidence confounding to the other children, for Inky was slow and weak, despicably smart, his kicking foot misshapen and inward turning, his face splotched with a birthmark that looked like an army of squid.

The other children could tell, just by looking at him, that there was a piece missing. He was the only kid anybody knew who could consistently strike out at the game of kick ball. Nobody wanted Inky as a teammate, not even his own older brother. Any other child would have cried, but Inky was very nearly all dried out.

As the players took their sides, and the line of kick-ball candidates shrank toward Inky alone, he realized that his brother Gilbert would choose him, not because he wanted him, but because he was the only one left.

All children grow, but Inky Mess was going to grow into something entirely different.

CHAPTER 1

CLEMENCY POGUE, fairy killer, conquering hero, globe-trotter, sometime bumblebee, tailor of burlap pants, and fast friend to hobgoblins, dogs, and needful children, was growing restless.

She had traveled the world, reanimating the fairies mistakenly murdered by her own misbelief. She had risked her life and she had earned victory, along with the respect and friendship of the hobgoblin Chaphesmeeso.

And had she not learned a bit of responsibility from all of this, Clem would have many times by now used Chaphesmeeso's name to call him simply to relieve her boredom. Her life suddenly seemed to suffer a significant scarcity of crisscrossing the globe with a hobgoblin sidekick in pursuit of extraordinary derring-do.

Clemency's life now was a series of extra ordinary derring-don'ts. See Clemency make porridge! Thrill as she stubs her toe on an Ottoman![1] Tremble in anticipation of lunch in a

---

[1] The footstool, not the tribe of Oghuz Turks in the fifteenth century Middle Eastern province of Anatolia.

brown bag . . . with carrot sticks!

Her adventure had left her sensitive to the world of the Make-Believe, but even those fairies and hobgoblins toiling at the edges of the waking world were humdrum at best. Clem spent the entirety of one social studies class watching the Fairy of Nothing Better to Do run into a window pane over and over again until she knocked herself unconscious and had to be carried off by the Head-Trauma Fairy.

Clemency had perfected her recipe for unbearably sweet, bubbly tea of sassafras root months before. Her father had dubbed the concoction "root beer," and though Clemency thought it wrong to call something so sweet such a bitter, yeasty thing, the name once given seemed impossible to lose.

Clemency understood the power of names, especially in the world of the Make-Believe. As with Rumpelstiltskin, a Make-Believe creature must obey any command given by a person who knows his name. It had been the Rumpelstiltskin Rule that had earned Clemency the service of the hobgoblin Chaphesmeeso. And it had been by her discovery of the name "Tinkasinge," the Fairy of Frequent and Painful Pointless

Antagonism, that Clemency had defeated the spiteful sprite and earned the magical ability to transform into a bee.

Bumbling with the bees eased her boredom at first but lost its appeal as she discovered that the only company to be had was bees. She quickly learned their language of dance but found that bees rarely had anything interesting to say.

"Can you believe all these blueberry blossoms?" she would dance. "The pollen does wonders for my vomit!" (Bees never danced the word "honey," but called the stuff by its place in their lives, "vomit." Her parents were not so charmed when Clemency asked for "bee vomit" to put on her popovers.)

"But the honeysuckle pollen," Clemency-Bee would dance, "pure nastiness. Who'd a thunk?"

"Lotta work to do," any bee would respond, and buzz off without pause. Clemency hadn't turned into a bee for weeks now. Ever since the chill of winter had set in, Clemency-Bee had discovered that it was easy to be chilled to the bone when you had an exoskeleton.

She turned to books. Mr. Pogue's volumes

were mostly instructional, concerning themselves with home remedies, woodworking, and cheesecraft. Mrs. Pogue's books were mostly about women who fell in love with either pirates or Gypsies, but Clemency couldn't read them without blushing so thoroughly that her head threatened to pop. Her school had a few choice volumes in its library, and Clemency gave several thorough readings to *The Tempest, The Goblin-Jar Tree, Frankenstein, The Hatter Bear,* and *The Epic of Gilgamesh*. But soon she had them all nearly memorized and there were no more diversions to be had.

On the long walk through the frosty afternoon forest, from the creaky wooden schoolhouse back to her kitten-warm cottage home, Clemency began to plot some trouble. She needed an excuse for adventure, some catastrophe that would justify calling Chaphesmeeso and attempting the impossible for a chance at the sublime. Maybe she could set fire to something or start an earthquake. If she could get her hands on a wombat, three vegetable peelers, and enough contact cement . . .

By the time she returned home, finished her homework, and began to cook dinner,

Clemency had worked out a plot so nefarious, cold, and sweet that it made her teeth hurt. Her forest home, the balance of the world, and Clemency's good reputation may all have been lost had not her parents tumbled home from work and unleashed an avalanche of boxer-dog pups.

The six grinning, warm little bundles broke loose from Mrs. Pogue's arms and swept across the floor toward Clemency, where she stood, wide-eyed, with a wooden spoon over a pot of pumpkin soup.

"Puppies!" she barely had a chance to shout before she was knocked off her feet and buried under gently scrabbling paws, baby-dog bellies as soft as a sultan's pajamas, furiously wagging pencil-thin tails, and tongues that flopped rakishly from mouths that dog-smiled so wide they'd have shamed clams.

Clemency laughed and rolled on the floor, trying to push the affectionate tongues from her face.

"Do you think you could take care of some puppies for a few weeks?" Mrs. Pogue asked, plucking the spoon from the pile of puppies and stirring the pot of simmering pumpkin.

"Yes!" Clemency shouted.

"We can find somebody else if you're busy," her father said, rummaging through the junk drawer.

"Yes! Yes!" Clemency shouted around dog kisses.

"You mean you want us to find somebody else?" her mom asked.

"I'll watch the puppies! I'll watch the puppies!" Clemency shouted, pulling the most affectionate boxer from her face and sitting up. He went limp in her arms and grinned at her with big, black eyes. The puppy was toffee brown with a splotch of white on his side shaped like a pair of boxer shorts. Like all the puppies, he had big floppy ears and a long, skinny tail.

Mr. Pogue found the enormous pair of scissors he had been looking for.

"His birthmark looks like boxer shorts," said Clemency. "Is that why they call them boxers?"

The puppy answered her question by raising his forepaws, jabbing with the left, and then delivering a roundhouse punch with the right that would have shattered Clemency's jaw if she were made of pastry.

PUPPIES!

"Henry," she said, "behave!"

"Careful, Clemency, don't name them," said her mother. "We have to give the puppies back."

It was too late. Now that she had said the name, she couldn't see Henry as anything else.

"Our boss asked us to raise the puppies away from their mom. He's going to give them to his friends in a few weeks," said Mr. Pogue, sharpening the scissors on a stone.

"Oh," Clemency said. Henry licked her nose.

"But we need you to take care of them in the meantime," said Mrs. Pogue.

"Done," Clemency said, hugging Henry.

"But first I need to take care of their tails and ears," said Mr. Pogue. Clemency saw the gleam of the scissors' edge and realized that her dad meant a whole different kind of "take care."

CHAPTER 2

MR. POGUE HELD a boxer puppy up off the kitchen table by the tip of a brown and white tail as thin and delicate as a child's pinky finger. The puppy grinned and wiggled at the attention. Mr. Pogue slid the open scissors in, a knuckle's distance from the base, until the tail rested against the crux of the two blades.

Then he squeezed.

Even from outside, Clemency and her mother could hear the yelp and the five that quickly followed.

Clemency had heard of "bobbing boxers" before but assumed it had something to do with fishing puppies from a barrel of water. Her mother explained that it meant cutting off their tails into stubby little nubbins and clipping the ears into triangular points. Mrs. Pogue said that it was tradition, and the millionaire who employed her and Mr. Pogue had demanded that his boxers be bobbed.

"Tails first, then ears," Mr. Pogue had said with forced cheer, ushering his wife and daughter outside so Clemency would not have to watch.

But Clemency could not bear more than six of the tiny yelps or the growing chorus of whimpers. She broke free of her mother's arms and ran into the house, where she found her teary-eyed father holding a terrified Henry by the scruff of his neck, a floppy ear draped over a scissors blade. Henry's left ear would be the first of all the dogs' to be cut.

Mr. Pogue squeezed.

"Dad!" Clemency shouted as Henry squealed.

Mr. Pogue looked up at Clemency, and the scissoring blades paused. They had nicked Henry's ear but not yet cut in deeply.

Mr. Pogue's lower lip quivered, and he dropped Henry and the scissors both. Henry scampered to Clemency, and she stooped and scooped him into her arms. She sat on the floor and all the other stub-tailed, floppy-eared puppies crawled miserably into her lap.

Now what will they wag when they're happy? Clemency wondered. It was not a question that would be answered that night.

* * *

Mr. Pogue put the tails in a shoe box to take to a friend of his who enjoyed fishing, but set them aside when Clemency asked if she could hold a funeral service for them, to help the puppies let go of their lost appendages.

Henry was crying and her parents were arguing the next morning when Clemency went to school. All day, she thought of the puppies as her teacher droned on, while the good Fairies of Deviated Septums and Crusty Sleeves attended to the dozens of children whose noses were running as fast as they could but still had been caught by the cold that was going around.

She ran home through the icebox forest, her breath pluming out behind her, as if she were a locomotive that chugged along to the rhythm of *puppies, puppies, puppies, puppies.*

Five of the boxer pups had regained their giddy joy of puppiness. They grinned, they yelped, they pooped in Mr. Pogue's galoshes and chased phantom tails. The little nubbins at the dogs' fundaments, freed of their extra burden, didn't wag so much as vibrate; they looked like turtles having seizures.

The sixth boxer pup, however, lay on the ground as mournful as a plucked duck. The white patch on his side did not so much resemble boxer shorts as it did a flag of surrender. Clemency lifted Henry off of the kitchen floor, and he hung despairingly in her arms. His nose was warm and dry, his sad eyes gummy with sleep sand, his puppy breath sour and raspy.

"Henry," Clemency said, and hugged him to her. She could not bear to leave him behind and so bundled him in a towel and took him up, along with a shovel and the box of tails, and headed out into the darkening forest.

She carried the shoe box as carefully as she could, but no matter how gently held, the tails jostled and shifted inside.

The ground was frozen and could not be dug. Clemency ended up walking much farther than she had anticipated, all the way to the bottom of the gorge, where the frozen creek lay and the ground was soft and sandy. Clemency kept Henry under her coat, and he was so warm that she barely felt the chill of the winter evening.

By the time she had dug deep enough down, the moon had risen above, and cold, silvery light reflected from the frozen water and frosted sand. She laid the box in the bottom of

THEY'RE ALIVE!

the hole, removed the lid, and looked down at the six dogless tails. She pulled Henry from her coat.

"Rest in peace, boxer-dog tails," she said. "I hope there are dog butts waiting for you in heaven." Then she asked Henry, "Would you like to say anything?"

Henry looked at Clemency, then down at the tails, then up at the moon, then he howled high and clear. Clemency's heart felt like somebody was squeezing lemon juice on it.

Clemency was afraid that the tears would freeze to her face if she let herself cry. She hugged Henry and pushed him back inside her coat, where he continued to howl. She picked up the shovel, lifted a scoop of moonlit sand, and dropped it into the hole.

The tails twitched. Clemency blinked.

She looked down into the grave, shovel in hand, and held her breath. Henry softly howled again. She could feel his mournful breath against her chest.

One tail, half-covered in sand, curled slowly. Then another. As Clemency watched, the tails slowly wiggled and shifted in their shoe-box coffin, sand scraping against cardboard.

"They're alive," she said. "Henry, they're alive!"

Henry softly coughed and rubbed his face between his paws.

CHAPTER 3

THE BOXER TAILS FORSOOK milk, hot chocolate, and even water, but suckled eagerly when Clemency fed them root beer from an eyedropper.

Clemency kept the shoe box hidden beneath her bed for several nights, but the pups mistrusted their own severed tails and growled so consistently through the night that Clemency eventually moved the box to the top of her closet.

Her parents were arguing more and more about the boxer pups' ears. Mrs. Pogue was certain that they would lose their jobs if they brought the young dogs back half-bobbed. When Mr. Pogue asked if she herself wanted to take up the scissors and cut their ears to match their tails, Mrs. Pogue grew silent.

Clemency did not tell them about her box of tails. It seemed one more puppy topic they might differ on, any number of muffled arguments she would have to pretend not to hear from the kitchen while she was lying in bed feigning sleep.

In three weeks, as spring began to scrape at Jack Frost, Clemency had house-trained the boxer pups, and even taught two of them to sit on command.

"That's amazing!" her father said.

"I'm amazing," Clemency had to admit.

The puppies were a force of adorable. They were endlessly eager, aggressively affectionate. They slept all jumbled together, like a basket of warm muffins, and woke at a run with grins on their faces.

All but Henry, who slept longer and longer hours, and when he woke, barely had the energy to lift a paw. He was ever squinting through eyes gummed with tears and sleep sand. He panted even when it was cool, for his chest and ears were burning hot. Clemency would hold him close and feed him warm milk from a bottle, but he could barely manage a sip.

As the weeks passed and Henry got no better, Clemency's heart slowly and steadily broke. When the morning came for Mr. Pogue to take Henry and the other five puppies back to the millionaire, the remainder of Clemency's fragile heart shattered to pieces and scattered like garnish over her spleen and gallbladder. Alone in the house, she added extra sugar to the root beer she was brewing for the tails, to mask the salty taste of her tears.

When her parents returned from work, Mr. Pogue was carrying a small bundle in one hand and his hat in the other. As Mrs. Pogue had predicted, the millionaire had fired him for failing to crop the boxers' ears.

He handed the bundle to Clemency. She pulled back the swaddling and found inside, sleepy and tender, Henry's wrinkled little face.

"Henry!"

"The millionaire wouldn't take him," said Mrs. Pogue. "He's a very sick puppy."

"We should take him to the doctor," Clemency said.

"A veterinarian looked at him," Mr. Pogue said, shaking his head. "He said there was nothing we could do. Henry has only a few days to live."

CHAPTER 4

CLEMENCY WAS NOT the kind to admit that there was nothing she could do. She barely slept the first evening of Henry's return home.

She looked through all of her parents' books for information on dog disease but ended up spending more time reading the dictionary for explanations of difficult words like "squamous"[2] or "zymosis."[3]

She held him bundled close to her chest and whispered to him to get better. She wiped the crusty yellow gum away from his eyes and tried to get him to drink a little water from the eye-dropper.

But she would have had better luck coaxing life into a cold potato. Henry was getting smaller and lighter. His paws curled up against his chest, under his tucked chin, and tiny hot breaths puffed weakly from his cold, dry nose.

Clemency cried carefully into her pillow so

[2] Scaly.
[3] An infectious disease.

as not to dampen Henry, who shivered against her in his fever.

By the time the sun rose, Henry had stopped shivering. Clemency had to put her ear to his chest in order to hear his faint, drowsy heartbeat.

Clemency needed hobgoblin help. She put on her burlap pants the way heroes do, leaping into them with both legs at once.

She packed her knapsack with books and a brown-bag lunch as if preparing for school and waited for her parents to leave for work. Mr. Pogue, however, remained in his bathrobe and offered to make waffles, as Mrs. Pogue trudged off into the morning cold.

"I lost my job for leaving floppy ears on the boxers," he reminded Clemency. "It's okay, honey, I'll find another one."

But it wasn't his unemployment that had cast a cloud over Clemency's mind. While her father was occupied with shaving, she fed the boxer tails their morning root beer, then carefully nestled Henry into the top of her knapsack.

"Off to school!" she shouted to her father, and walked out into the forest.

***

"Chaphesmeeso," she said softly once she was away from her house and well off the path to school. Her effort produced nothing but a frosty puff of breath.

"Chaphesmeeso," she said a little louder, "Come away to me." She knelt by her knapsack and stroked Henry's face. She said to the puppy, "He'll come, he'll help us."

She put an ear to the ground but heard nothing. "Drad nastit, hobgoblin, where are you? Chaphesmeeso, come here!" she said more forcefully.

She balled her fists as if squeezing the juice from hamsters, tears of frustration glimmering in her eyes. "Chaphe, you lazy, no-account, unprofessional fink of a goblin!"

Then she sat on the frozen ground, a little ways off from where it promptly exploded.

"You forgot the *hob*," he said, stepping from a shower of falling earth. "*Fink*, yes. *Lazy*, proudly. But, and this is important, I am a *hob*-goblin, not a goblin. Hobgoblins maintain order, the balance. Goblins are nothing but chaos and nastiness, toe-jam sandwiches and— AH! AH! HUG! STOP HUGGING!"

Chaphesmeeso's arms waved frantically

behind Clemency as she squeezed him in her arms.

"I missed you," she said. "I need help."

"Less hugging!" he cried.

Clemency let him go and he shook like a wet dog.

"You got affection all over me!" He wiped at his gourd-skinned belly as if sluicing off leeches, then pinky-reamed the pig ears atop his head and wrung out the rabbit ears beneath them, stomping his hog legs on the ground. Leaning conspiratorially forward so that the dwarfish figure behind him would not hear, he said softly to Clemency, "It's good to see you, too."

Clemency smiled only for a moment. Behind Chaphe there was what appeared to be a pale, filthy, mud-streaked boy of seven or eight, dressed as a hobgoblin.

"You brought a friend," she said.

"Hi! You can call me Kennethurchin," the boy said, then added in a whisper, "but it's not my real name. We dug all the way here from Katmandu! And I helped!"

"I'm Clemency."

"Ignore him, and don't stick any forks in

him," said Chaphesmeeso. "He's not done yet, not until we find his proxy."

The boy grinned enormously and silently mouthed the word "sorry." Clemency wondered what his proxy could possibly look like; Kennethurchin himself already looked like a poor substitute for a hobgoblin. His boots and pointy metal hat could have come off the anvil of the same zealous blacksmith who pounded out Chaphe's, but the resemblance ended there. He was a costumed human boy, with a head shaped like a chestnut and the look about him of a prince frog, as if possessed of the noblest stature so tiny and slimy a creature could attain.

"Is that a boy or a goblin? I mean *hob*goblin," Clem asked.

"Half of each but less than both combined. And until he chooses, he's my bird's armpit," Chaphe said.

"He means he's taken me under his wing," Kennethurchin whispered, explaining. "It's really rather clever."

"Hush, doughboy, you're embarrassing me," said Chaphesmeeso. "Besides, she's sharp enough to pop it herself."

"Chaphe . . . ," said Clem before the hob-goblin's hoary hand clamped over her mouth.

"Hey, careful," said Chaphe, "no need to give the world my name, invite them to slip a puppeteer's hand where it's fundamentally unwelcome. Here I thought our last fairy-slaughtering globe-trot had taught you a little restraint in meddling in the Make-Believe."

"She knows your name? You're not supposed to let *anybody* know your name!" said Kennethurchin.

"Reel in your gast, it's flabbering. I told you, little Miss Fishhook here is only round on the outside." Chaphesmeeso turned his basset hound-weary eyes on Clemency. "I'll be highly disappointed if you use my name for anything but an apoplectically apocalyptic pickle. Or better yet, a calamity gherkin; my time is unfashionably short. It so happens that I'm in the middle of a quest to find this boy-goblin halfling's clay-baby changeling before he makes mincemeat of the Make-Believe and mutton of this mutt." He hooked a hoary thumb at Kenn.

Clemency nodded and took a shuddering breath.

"My dog is sick," she said.

Chaphesmeeso, who never looked impressed, nearly had to lie down to show how specifically unimpressed he was.

"Did I not mention the total annihilation of Make-Believe existence that this half mooncalf and I were hoping to prevent?" Chaphe asked. "Every fairy-whisper across the globe is predicting a hundred percent chance of doom with a high probability of despair if we fail in our noble quest."

"Um, hob sir?" Kennethurchin was crouched over Clem's knapsack, looking in at the wrinkled little bundle clinging by a silkworm's thread to life. "Her puppy really does look sick."

"I eat puppies for breakfast. Where's the milk?" said Chaphesmeeso, glancing over at the knapsack.

"His name's Henry," Clemency said.

Chaphesmeeso looked at the sick puppy as if he had nearly stepped in it. The hobgoblin cocked his head to the side, and his rabbit ears quivered, picking out distant signals from the wind.

"Clem," he said, "there's nothing we can do. Every fairy-whisper says he's got three paws in the grave."

"There's always something we can do," Clemency said. "You and me together are unstoppable."

"We do okay," Chaphe admitted, "but that's not a puppy, that's dog-shaped fertilizer. If you're looking for a quest, help me find the changeling, destroy it, and save the Make-Believe and this halfling's sanity."

"I can risk crazy a little longer," said Kenn, looking affectionately at Henry.

"Please," said Clemency.

Chaphe looked back at Henry, who, with several of his last ounces of will, opened one droopy eye.

Any hobgoblin hates to admit that there is a heart anywhere in his torso other than one he ate in a chowder, but as Chaphesmeeso glanced at one very sick puppy, some lub-dubbing thing inside him softened just a little bit.

"Poop," said the hobgoblin.

CHAPTER 5

KENNETHURCHIN'S CHANGELING was alive and well, motherless and miserable, and unaware that he carried the potential for the end of the Make-Believe.

Inky lay awake in bed, staring at his sleeping brother in the neighboring bed and stewing over the kick-ball game he had endured that afternoon. Gilbert had given him the least important position on the whole field, Second Catcher, but still Inky managed to find a way to lose the game for the entire team.

When it came Inky's time at the plate, he had missed the ball and kicked home base instead, sending the base skittering across the field. So when Gilbert tried to steal home and win the game, he found the base missing and the catcher waiting with the ball to tag him out. The entire opposing team had laughed, while Inky's own teammates glowered at him as he returned to the bench with his head bent low from the weight of shame.

"Why do you have to be so . . ." Gilbert

moved his mouth around as if trying to regurgitate something large and nasty without letting it touch his tongue, finally spitting out the word, "weird!"

Inky never slept. His nights were like cold molasses, slow and dark, but sweet in the loneliness they offered. Only recently had he discovered how truly strange this was. Other children would talk about sleep, thrilling and frightening Inky, who having never slept himself, thought of it like an imitation of death.

And dreams! Inky boiled quietly with envy of everyone else's ability to dream. Other children in the night flew, swam as dolphins, played canasta with yeti, harvested marshmallow fields, or buzzed with the bees in spring. Inky stewed alone in the darkness.

A little cold molasses was not such a bad idea. He slipped out of bed and crept into the kitchen.

Inky had an insatiable sweet tooth, difficult to please in a family that earned its bread by pickles. Mess Brand Pickles were in stores throughout the Carolinas, a family recipe Gilbert and Inky's father toiled at tirelessly, single-handedly turning out epic pecks of pickles from the giant vats of vinegar he kept in the barn.

The kitchen leaped into sharp, orange relief when Inky lit his candle, sparking a tiny metallic gleam that he caught from the corner of his eye, gone when he turned to look. Inky set the candle on an overturned pickle-jar lid on the kitchen table, then quietly dragged a chair to the pantry.

For more than a month, he had visited the molasses as regularly as if courting it, and less than an inch remained in the bottom of the jar. Mouth watering, finger scooping through the thick, sticky darkness, he caught again a glimpse of glimmering mote.

Inky froze, only his eyes slowly rotating toward the candle. The glimmer was a reflection off of a tiny metal rod, held in the tiny hand of a tiny woman with wings. She seemed transfixed by the candle, floating in the air a few inches from the flame.

A fairy. The tiny creatures had been on the edges of his vision as long as he could remember. He had learned to pretend to ignore them, knowing that seeing fairies would only mean more mockery. But never had he seen one so close or so clearly.

INTERESTING...

Very slowly, Inky took his finger from the molasses. He rotated the jar in his hands so that its mouth pointed downward; molasses began to creep down its sides.

The fairy moved closer to the candle, her gossamer wings throwing cotton candy-colored light on Inky, like diluted stained glass. She stayed just far enough from the candle to avoid burning, just within the circumference of the overturned pickle-jar lid.

Inky pounced. He leaped from the chair, crossed the kitchen as fast as a shadow, slammed the upside-down jar onto the lid, and twisted it fast. A dollop of molasses snuffed the candle flame. The kitchen fell into darkness but for a faint glow inside the molasses-streaked jar.

Inky lit a match and held it close to the glass. The fairy was inside, furious, fluttering, and streaked with sticky, sweet darkness.

"Interesting," said Inky. He licked the molasses from his finger.

CHAPTER 6

CLEMENCY AND CHAPHESMEESO left Kennethurchin behind to take care of Henry and the boxer tails. She told him to keep the puppy warm and explained how to feed the boxer tails root beer from an eyedropper.

"You'll have to sneak around my dad," Clemency warned.

"Nah," said Chaphe, "Kenn's Make-Believe enough that grown-ups won't see him. I should be so lucky to be so blind."

"You're pretty mean to Kennethurchin," Clem said.

"The cuter he gets, the hobgoblinier he ain't," Chaphe said, watching the boy walk toward the Pogue cottage, cradling the puppy in his arms with obvious tenderness.

"What are we gonna do for Henry?" Clemency asked.

"The answer to that's on the far side of the world," said Chaphe.

"Are you still fast?" Clemency asked.

"As a hunger artist. I could put a girdle

round about the earth in four minutes, then tighten it and make the trip again in three. Hobgoblin, will travel; you know the drill and how to get it spinning." He leaned forward, offering his rabbit ears.

Clemency took one in each hand and lifted him from the ground. Chaphe flipped over with the weight of his pointy metal helmet.

"Nice pants," he said, and then they dropped into the earth like a stone into water.

Fltftftftftftftftftftft! Chaphesmeeso's arms, tunneling furiously, made a sound like a wood-pecker demolishing nougat. Clemency held fast to Chaphe's ears as they rocketed downward, tunneling through soil and rock with equal ease, gravity rotating around Clemency as they passed the midway point within a matter of seconds, all of a sudden tunneling upward.

A small geyser of dirt and cement exploded with them as they burst upward from the earth and into a dark, windy tunnel that rumbled like a thousand bowling alleys.

Clemency shook the dirt from her hair and looked around. Cement pebbles pattered like rain around them in a tunnel of near pitch-darkness slowly giving way to an approaching light.

The rumbling was growing louder. Clemency had the distinct impression of being in the guts of a cement giant suffering indigestion. The source of light became more distinct past the curve in the tunnel a short distance away, roaring and screeching now, shaking loose dirt from the ceiling.

"Always a crapshoot digging into New York," said Chaphesmeeso. "Though at least we didn't run into any crap chutes. You'll want to lie down and hold still."

"Why?" Clemency asked. She looked over, and Chaphesmeeso was already prone across the filthy wooden beams, between two metal rails. It looked as if somebody had laid an enormous ladder along the tunnel floor.

A light of realization fell across Clemency. Scratch that—it was the light of an onrushing subway train as it rounded the corner. She turned into the glare, throwing her shadow over the reclining hobgoblin behind her.

"Ah," said Clemency, and dropped to the ground between the rails a moment before the train roared over her, the cars clattering black and enormous like an iron tornado. Clemency put her fingers in her ears, careful not to stick her elbows up where they would get pulverized by the axles whipping past her like steel baseball bats.

It was over in a matter of seconds, the train passed them as suddenly as it had arrived, the relative quiet in the tunnel a storm of silence. Chaphesmeeso was on his feet, shaking the dirt from his ears.

Clemency got up and screamed until she ran out of breath.

"Feeling better?" Chaphesmeeso asked.

Clemency inhaled, then asked, "What are we going to do for Henry?"

"Ah. You've got a broken puppy, but take him to a human doctor to get fixed and you'll just have a broken puppy who's more comfortable riding a bicycle." Chaphe led through the tunnel, stepping from tie to tie, Clemency close on his heels. "So we'll find the vital fairy, here being one occupied by a cat's diaphragm; mysterious since the imp in question is the Fairy of Very Sick Puppies."

They emerged from the tunnel, climbed up onto the subway platform, and ignored the scream of a businessman waiting for the next train.

"Is there a child involved?" Clem asked.

"There's always a child involved," said Chaphe. "In this case, a girl named Anna, puckered face, pickled heart, a year your senior, daughter to the owner of a used bookshop where she's often left in charge while her parents refuse to come out from under the sheets and covers of the books they sell."

"And her problem?" Clem asked.

"Her cat's got the hiccups."

"So we cure the hiccups, and the fairy's free to help Henry," said Clem.

Chaphe put a finger to the tip of his prodigious nose.

"One thing doesn't add up," Clemency said.

"Why a *kitten* plus hiccups equals a visit from the Fairy of Very Sick *Puppies*?" Chaphe suggested.

"Right." said Clemency as they climbed the stairs toward the light.

"Hence the mystery," said Chaphe.

They emerged into daylight and noise.

"Holy Toledo," said Clemency.

"Not even close," said Chaphe. They were in the middle of a city bigger than any exclamation.

CHAPTER 7

NEW YORK CITY was like an incalculably complex clockwork contraption of incredibly coordinated chaos, yellow taxis, kamikaze pigeons, people moving and darting like brilliant fish, shouts, music, and the jangle of coins careening through a canyon of buildings that could have served as the ceremonial armor of stone giants.

"Close your mouth; some pigeons might roost," Chaphesmeeso said. Clemency managed to lift her jaw but continued to stare up at the glimmering towers.

"This is the best place ever," she said.

"Suretainly. Though it's hard to find good Mexican food. Bookshop yonder." He waddled off between the cross-rushing swarms of very important people. Clemency scrambled after, bumped and jostled by more people in half a minute than she had seen in the prior month.

A filthy hand reached out of the crowd and grabbed Clemency's arm.

"Take me back!" said a raspy, slurred voice. "Brain-mites. Cancer-crab-crust. Tell him to take me back underground!" Clemency thought at first that the owner of the voice was a bear made of garbage. But it was a human, a man, as old as her father but infinitely more worn. His skin was as grime streaked and mealy as soggy bread. He smelled like the bathroom after grandmother had been eating cats, and his eyes rolled with a miserable panic of insanity.

He was staring at Chaphesmeeso.

"Skin-beetles! Take me back!" he said.

"He can see you," Clemency said.

Chaphe pulled the homeless man's hand off of Clemency's arm. "Come away from him; you might slip on his dropped marbles."

"Please, help me! Goblins-whisper-ocean-floor-giants. Take me back! Take me under-ground," the man said.

Clemency did not know whether she felt more sympathy or fear.

"He's off his rocker; he's not even on the porch anymore," Chaphe said. "That's a not-gob, a grown-up boy who didn't get his goblin name. That's what's waiting for Kenn if we can't find his changeling. Hobgoblins in train-ing who don't make the grade get kicked above ground and lost to the insanity clause."

"The what?"

"You don't believe insanity clause?" Chaphe pulled Clemency away, frantic New Yorkers quickly spilling between them and the homeless man.

"Get your head straight," Chaphe said. "There's a puppy waiting on you."

Chaphe was right. Clemency thought of Henry and put her brain back to the job at hand.

The bookshop had a dusty, glass-fronted door that read GRAHAM, GRAHAM, & DAUGHTER; USED AND RARE BOOKS. A tin cowbell chimed as Clemency stumbled through the door, Chaphesmeeso slipping in behind.

In the muffled library silence of the shop, teetering stacks of dusty books imitated the city outside, forming towering canyons that tottered precariously overhead. The titles looming over Clemency were a sore temptation; there were hundreds more books in this little shop than she could have read if given years.

Scrrrrrrt, Hick, Hick, Hick, Scrrrrrrrt, Hick, Hick. A slow, rasping samba was playing from the back of the store, the *scrrrrrrt!* of old paper tearing, punctuated like a barn dance with rhythmic *hick*s!

"What's that sound?" whispered Clemency.

"No way to find out but to creep and peep. Let's get this over with, all this human magic heebs my jeebies."

"The books?" Clemency asked, smiling up at the dusty tomes.

Chaphesmeeso nodded, scratching his belly anxiously.

"It's not really magic. I could teach you to read someday," Clemency offered.

"Not in a million years. That's strictly human magic, you and your thumbs and your eyes and your big brains all clustered to those spines," he said, looking up at the rows of books as if they were sleeping dragons.

"Let's get to work; we've got a sick puppy waiting," Clemency said, moving back toward the *Scrrrrt, Hick, Hick, Hick* . . . that continued from the back of the shop.

Anna was a round child with pigtailed hair and the eyes of a silencing librarian. She was sipping condensed milk from a can. *Hick, Hick, Hick* continued from nearby.

Clemency and Chaphesmeeso spied her

through the gap between a row of books and the shelf above.

"Fairy ho," said Chaphe, sighting a tiny figure buzzing anxious circles around Anna's head as Anna set aside the condensed milk and took up the nearest book.

Anna flipped through the old leather-bound volume, its thick pages releasing small swarms of dust mites that swirled in the dim light. She came to the last page, gripped it firmly by its corner, and—*Scrrrrt!*—ripped it free from the binding.

Clemency's breath caught in her throat. She had never thought to do such a thing, and now to witness it nearly sickened her. Anna smiled as if she had just swallowed the last cookie in the jar, and dropped the page into a huge green garbage bin filled with such final words.

"Stop that!" said Clemency. Anna was so preoccupied that she did not even look up but simply reached for the next book.

"She's a monster," Clemency whispered.

"And there the monster's cat in its conniption," said Chaphe, nodding farther back in the store where an orange tabby twitched and bucked, *Hick! Hick!* each hiccup doubling it like an inchworm.

The cat's name tag read HAMMETT. He was hiccuping too frequently to flee from the girl and the hobgoblin.

"Hold his ears while I make him drink some water," Clemency said. "It always works for me."

"Hick! Hick!" said Hammett the cat.

"Scrrrrrt!" said a mutilated book behind them, making Clemency cringe.

"Where are you gonna divine a glass of water?" Chaphesmeeso asked, holding the twitching cat by the points of its ears.

"Hick!" said Hammett the cat.

"Hmm. Good point," Clemency said. "You got any ideas?"

Chaphesmeeso smiled.

"May I?" he asked.

Clemency nodded, and Chaphesmeeso lifted the cat to his face.

"I'M GOING TO EAT YOUR BRAIN WITH A SPOON AND CLEAN MY TEETH WITH YOUR SPINAL CORD! BLEAAARGH!" he shouted, threading his tongue in one nostril and out the other, rolling his eyes back, and crinkling his rabbit ears like lightning bolts.

SCRRRIT-HIC

"Hick!" said the unimpressed cat. "Hick!"

"Well, that didn't work." Chaphesmeeso grimaced, looking past the cat, toward Clemency. "I thought maybe—I'LL INFLATE YOUR SPLEEN AND PLAY A CAT-FIDDLE FUNERAL DIRGE ON YOUR GUTS! BLEAAARGH! BLEA, BLEA, BLEEAA-AAAAAARGH!" Chaphesmeeso stretched his mouth wide enough to halve his head, his teeth rioting like a prison-break, tongue and ears tied in knots, nostrils flaring like angry cobras.

"Hick!" said the cat, eyelashes thoroughly unbatted.

"This is not an easily scared cat," said Chaphesmeeso.

"Scrrrrt!" said a book protesting the loss of its last page.

"If she doesn't stop doing that, I'm going to smash her," said Clemency.

"Don't get distracted," Chaphe said. "There's a sick puppy waiting on our quest."

"There's a sick puppy mutilating books in her own . . ." Clemency trailed off, her eyes flashing with realization. She pointed at Hammett and said, "There's a cat with hiccups, and . . ."—she pointed at Anna—"*there* is a very sick puppy!"

"I'd buy it," said Chaphe.

"Hick!" said Hammett, and swatted Chaphesmeeso's nose.

"Ouch!" said Chaphe, and put the cat's head in his mouth.

"Stop that!" Clemency said as the cat's hind legs scrabbled furiously against Chaphe's chin.

"Stoff wuff?" Chaphe said.

"Scrrrrt!" said another book robbed of its ending.

"I'm going to smash you!" Clemency cried, and ran to the counter where Anna perched. "What's wrong with you?"

Anna looked up, blinking, noticing Clemency for the first time.

"Can I help you find a book?" she said.

"I'm not here to buy a book! What's wrong with you?" Clem demanded again.

Anna blinked.

"Why are you tearing the last pages from all these books?!" Clem said.

Anna sniffed and reached for her condensed milk.

"Nobody will know how they end!" Clemency shouted.

Anna's smile was slight and sly. "I will," she said.

Clemency looked upward, exasperated. Her eyes fell upon the Fairy of Very Sick Puppies, who returned her gaze with a look that said, *Go on, throttle her, I would if my hands were big enough.*

"That's not right!" Clemency said to Anna. "It's selfish and stupid!"

"Why do you care?" said Anna. "You're not here for a book."

"No, I'm here for my puppy," said Clemency, staring down at the counter in consternation. Her eyes fell on a grand dictionary, the frayed edges of the remnants of its final page protruding slightly.

"Ooh, I love dogs!" said Anna. "I have a cat, his name is Hammett. Here, kitty, kitty, kitty!"

Hammett could barely hear Anna from inside the hobgoblin's morass of a mouth.

"What's your puppy's name?" Anna asked.

Clemency looked up at Anna, then back down at the dictionary. She had an idea.

"My puppy's name is Henry, and he's in terrible trouble. He has an awful zymosis," she said.

"What's a zymosis?" Anna asked.

Clemency blinked.

"What's wrong with your puppy? What's a zymosis?" Anna asked again.

Clemency took the condensed milk from the counter and took a sip.

Anna snorted, fumed for an instant, then grabbed the dictionary from the counter.

"Fine!" she said, flipping through the pages. "I'll find it myself."

She flipped to the end and found that her dictionary ended at "Zorille,"[4] followed by the torn edge of a page she had ripped with her own hand.

Anna looked up at Clemency, jaw clenched like a bulldog's. They locked eyes for a moment, everyone relieved that neither was carrying six-shooters. Then Anna leaped to her feet, turned to the enormous green trash bin, and began frantically to search through it.

The Fairy of Very Sick Puppies heaved a relieved sigh and buzzed gratefully down to Clemency.

"Are you free to help me now?" Clem asked.

The fairy nodded.

[4] A North African muishond.

"Chaphe, take me home!" Clemency called out.

Chaphesmeeso turned toward them, nodded, and spat out the cat.

It took nearly half an hour for Hammett the cat to lick all the hobgoblin spit from his head and shoulders. He did not realize until he was done that he had not hiccuped once the whole time.

CHAPTER 8

THEY EXPLODED FROM the earth and into the forest, Clemency releasing Chaphesmeeso's ears, and the Fairy of Very Sick Puppies releasing the cuff of Clemency's pant leg.

The fairy alighted on a branch and began to brush the dirt gently from her wings.

Clemency grabbed the fairy and ran toward her house.

"Come on!" she shouted to Chaphesmeeso. Within sight of home, the urgency to bring her very sick puppy and the fairy together was nearly unbearable.

She did not notice Chaphesmeeso standing awkwardly over the hole behind her, not following. She thought of Henry's sleepy little eyes and tiny paws and was suddenly struck with the dread that possibly the fairy in her balled fist could only help the kind of Very Sick Puppies that stand on two legs.

She burst into her home, startling her father so that he dropped his cheese, and sprinted back to her room before he barely had a chance to say, "Clemency?"

She opened her own door more gently and entered her room, releasing the fairy.

Kennethurchin, sitting splay-legged on Clemency's bed, looked up from the swaddled bundle on his lap. His cheeks had been washed clean with tears, and still there was a quaver in his voice.

"He died. Right after you left, Henry died."

CHAPTER 9

KENNETHURCHIN SAT WEEPING on the bed, limp as a rag doll, as Clemency gently took the bundle from him. He leaned into her, crying helplessly, and she took his hand and held it.

"Clemency? Why are you home?" Her dad poked his head in the door, completely ignoring the weeping boy-goblin on the bed.

Clemency did not cry over Henry's death until her father took her in his arms and said how sorry he was.

Chaphesmeeso paced around the cottage, fists balled and face to the ground, shaking his head.

Mr. Pogue marveled at how easily the frozen earth in the garden behind the cottage was dug, still unwilling to see Kennethurchin, whose hobgoblin-trained fingers easily pulled apart the cold ground.

Henry's body was light in Clemency's arms. She kept a tight hold on him, suddenly struck by a fear that a breeze could carry him away.

She put Henry in the ground, and when her

dad waited for her to speak, she said, "Good dog. I love you, Henry."

She put her arm around Kennethurchin, who wept so much that he could barely stand, as Mr. Pogue shoveled dirt into the grave.

It was a comfort to Kennethurchin to care for the boxer tails, and his eyes dried for a few minutes as he held the shoe box in his lap and nursed them root beer.

But the sixth boxer tail, Henry's, lay cold and dead on the cardboard.

They took it into the garden to bury it by its dog.

"We have to go," Chaphesmeeso said, ceasing the pacing which had nearly worn a moat around Clemency's home. "Clemency, I'm no good at . . ."

For once, the hobgoblin was without words, and he simply squeezed Clemency's hand. She began to cry again.

Chaphesmeeso coughed and grumbled, trying to clear the lump from his throat.

"I should have pureed that frog," Chaphe weakly excused.

"We have to find my changeling," Kennethurchin said.

Chaphesmeeso released Clemency's hand and nodded. "He could destroy us all."

Clemency watched them walk into the woods and drop down into the earth, something like Henry had done, but different, because they could come back again.

CHAPTER 10

"I WISH . . . I WISH I could read," Inky Mess murmured to the jar of fairies as quietly as if he were wishing for fishnet stockings. All five fairies, glowing furiously in a jar the size of a watermelon, looked at Inky like he was a fart in church.

He had attempted the wish dozens of times, near hourly every sleepless night. Like Inky, and every Make-Believe creature, the fairies never slept. He had captured most of them at night, by the glow of a candle flame, his hope scraped more painfully new with each additional fairy.

"I wish I could read," he said more forcefully. "Help me!"

He could not have known that he had captured the Fairy of Motherless Children, the Fairy of Impossible Itches, the Fairy of Navel Hygiene, the Papercut Fairy, and the Fairy of Lost Things Found; even if they had been able to reach him through the glass, even if they had felt something other than fairy-pure rage at their captor, none of them had the skill to grant his specific wish.

Inky let the burlap fall over the jar, smothering its glow, and looked at the warning posted on the largest of the pickle barrels.

The bold red words swam and blurred under his gaze.

"I hate you," he said, unsure even himself whether he was talking to the words evading his understanding or his own reflection in the shiny copper barrel.

Inky knew he was smarter than other children; he could repeat all of his history lessons nearly word-for-word and solved in his head the math problems responsible for Einstein's hairstyle. Yet as the other seven- and eight-year-olds took to reading and writing as if made for it, Inky stared helplessly at pages of letters that twisted and bubbled before his eyes like slugs in salt.

Spoken words too had been difficult for Inky at first. Only by sheer will had he beaten and mastered the words that fit so awkwardly in his mouth. His very name had come about from the troublesome word "Kenneth," the name his mother gave him before she vanished.

When he tried to say "Kenny," the closest he could manage was "Inky."

Funny names, he had discovered, were sticky as spitballs, especially with a big brother in the picture.

An eye doctor (Inky knew the word was "ophthalmologist," though he could not have spelled it to save his life) had confused Inky's difficulty with letters for nearsightedness and prescribed him glasses that made the entire world a blurry haze.

Inky crept back to his room to retrieve his glasses, careful not to wake Gilbert. In the moonlit kitchen, he put the glasses on his face and pulled from his pajama breast pocket the many-folded piece of paper he carried with him always.

He stared at the letters on the creased page, squinting furiously at the wriggling black lines through the thick lenses.

Gilbert had given his little brother the letter a month earlier, in response to Inky's ceaseless pestering about their mom.

"But did she say where she went?" Inky asked for the umpteenth time.

"Shut up," Gilbert said.

"But she can't have just vanished," Inky said.

"Yeah she coulda. 'Cause she did." Gilbert gave Inky a little shove. "You're not old enough to know what happened."

"Am, too," Inky said.

Gilbert had devised a solution as casually cruel as only older brothers know how.

"When you're old enough to read, you'll be old enough to know what happened to mom," he had said, scribbling the story of their mother across the sheet of paper.

Gilbert was a strong reader but claimed to hate it, a combination that confounded and infuriated Inky.

Inky had stared at the writing on the paper for hours each of the dozens of nights since Gilbert had authored it, but the letters refused to cooperate.

The world simply was not fair. Inky was without friends, rest, dreams, and books, so many things that other children took as naturally as air. But there was one thing every child has and that Inky would not be denied: a mother.

CHAPTER 11

IT WAS THE DREAM-HEAVY hours before dawn.

Darling, sweet in swaddling clothes,
Hear not the creep that creaks the floor.
Goblins wait for tired eyes to close,
Then drag you 'neath, a child no more.

In Clemency's dreams, she was frozen, help-less in the corner of a nighttime nursery, watch-ing some terrible thing, like a child scarecrow made of beef jerky steal quietly toward a sleeping baby. It was frightening and awful and . . . it rhymed. She decided to wake up.

She opened her eyes to a face as ugly as a boiled bulldog, its teeth bared as if for a bloody midnight snack.

"Were you whispering nightmares into my ear?" Clemency asked.

"Who, me? Were you scared?" Chaphesmeeso asked.

"Not even a little bit," lied Clemency, sitting up. Chaphe's feelings looked honestly hurt, so she relented. "Okay maybe a little. But I'm extra tough, so even a little scared is pretty impressive."

She rubbed the sleep sand from her eyes. Weeks had passed since Henry's death, and the empty space it had left inside Clemency, though not filled, was at least starting to smooth over.

"What's the story?" she said.

"My abecedarian is AWOL," said Chaphe.

"Um," said Clemency.

"My flunky rookie's playing hooky," said Chaphe.

"Kennethurchin," said Clem. "He's missing?"

Chaphe put a finger to his nose. "Bull's-eye proboscis. He gushed so much about those boxer-dog tails of yours that I started wishing he'd dry up and blow off, then blow and behold he did."

Behind Chaphesmeeso, hovering on wings like glass scalpels, there was a childlike, pot-bellied fairy just barely visible in the dark bedroom. Her skin was a midnight blue, smooth and plump as an overripe berry. Her eyes and the tip of her wand were blue like the base of a candle flame. Clemency felt immediately that she wanted to get as far from the fairy as possible.

LONG GOODNIGHTS

"Normally I'd applaud with pigs, clappy as a ham to see the dwindling lights of Kennethurchin's caboose. But then of course there's this grand adventure in the balance of which hangs all the Make-Believe, this fairy black hole, though you probably wouldn't want to hear about that . . . ," Chaphesmeeso said temptingly.

The eyes of the midnight blue fairy had attracted a small moth, who fluttered clumsy circles around her.

"Who's that fairy?" Clemency asked.

"That," said Chaphe, "is a fairy across a river from which nobody returns. The Fairy of Long Goodnights, who knows a lullaby that more than lulls, and no child hears twice."

As Chaphesmeeso spoke, the Fairy of Long Goodnights reached out her wand and casually touched the fluttering moth. The fine powder coating fell from the moth's wings in a soft puff of color. Clemency gasped. The denuded veins of the moth's wings would certainly have embarrassed the poor insect had not it been instantly struck dead, spiraling to the ground like a leaf.

"If all the Make-Believe were good, we'd

get bored," Chaphesmeeso explained. "Besides, she's key to our quest. A dearth of death no awfully big adventure makes. And Kennethurchin and I, if I can find the daft draft of a hobgoblin, are engaged on the awfullest and biggest adventure of all. But you wouldn't want to hear about that, would you?" Chaphesmeeso said as Clemency peered into the top of her closet.

"They're gone, the boxer-dog tails. He must have taken them," she said, then grabbed a stub of candle from her bedside. "Come on."

There was still a chill in the Springtime night, and Clemency's breath puffed in the glow of the candle. She zigged and zagged, dodging the Fairy of Long Goodnights, who kept circling around her, seemingly transfixed.

"You short for Oklahoma?" Chaphesmeeso asked, waddling along behind her.

"I'm okay. Just tell this fairy I'm not interested in any permanent naps," Clemency said.

"Don't get your funeral shroud in a bunch; you've an admirable shine, but you don't hold a candle to the candle you're holding. Fairies get addle-brained by candle flames; they love 'em like sugar. It's the reason you put the things on birthday cakes to attract wishes. Fire-gifted fairies will relight them till they're snuffed in the icing."

Clemency held the candle as far from herself as she could, and they continued into the forest.

They found Kennethurchin by the sound of his chuckling, in the shadow of the great oak tree whose roots hung over the edge of a deep gorge, where Clemency and Chaphesmeeso had first met so seemingly long ago.

The boxer tails had grown to the size of garden snakes, almost too large for their shoe box. Kenn had them in a hollow between oak roots, laughing softly and whispering to the five tails that squirmed and wriggled around his hands.

"Clemency!" he said. "It's good to see you, oh, gosh, I hope you don't mind that I borrowed your boxer-dog tails, but the thing of it is, is that my mentor"—he nodded to Chaphesmeeso—"is kind of mean and I needed to be cheered up and dogs cheer me up but your dog makes me sad 'cause he's dead and that made me think of the box of mmmf hmmmf mmm mmmfm mmm."

Kenn's words had built up enough inertia

that Chaphe's hand clamped over his mouth could only muffle the sound as the rest unsaid piled up and crashed.

"The gob on this half hob. I've met quieter and wiser roosters . . ." said Chaphe, taking his hand from Kenn's face as if his mouth were a loaded bear trap, ". . . and fried them. Thanks for helping me find him, Clem, if one thanks another for helping him restore the boil to his bottom."

That's me, Kenn silently mouthed before his attention strayed back down to the boxer-dog tails. He suddenly seemed to Clemency more boy than hobgoblin, and she thought of how exhausting his life of constant tunneling must be.

"You really love those tails, don't you?" she said.

"Oh, yes. They're my favorite in the whole world."

"Your favorite amputated, reanimated dog tails?" Chaphe asked.

Kenn nodded.

"Well—" Clemency paused. The tails had been a comfort since Henry's death, but Kennethurchin clearly had a need. "They're yours."

Kenn smiled like he was made of sugar.

"You should give them names," Clemency said.

"Oh, no," Kennethurchin said, "only the Tallygob gives names."

"Who?" Clemency asked.

"The Tallygob," said Chaphe, "the one-shy-of-extinct Eponymous Rex, keeper of the Forgetting Book, oldest of hobgoblins. The self-same hob who gave us our grand and epic quest to find the lost fairies, rescue Kenn's sanity, and restore balance to the whole Make-Believe, which you probably don't care about. So now that I have my five-tailed ass and midnight fairy, we can embark anew on our sure-to-be-legendary adventure. I'm sure you wouldn't want to tag along; and if we cannot add you, then *adieu*."

"Okay," said Clemency, "what's this adventure?"

"I told you she'd help us," said Kennethurchin.

CHAPTER 12

"THE CRISIS COMMENCED," said Chaphesmeeso, "when my half-hob heel here was denied a goblin name by the Forgetting Book. His changeling, you see, bailed out on the baleful bath that renders proxy preemies to clay-baby soup. So we've lost the life-giving Leviathan Ink that would make Kennethurchin a hobgoblin."

"Uh-huh," said Clemency.

"A fairy web was cast far and wide to find the fugitive changeling. But the searchers only found themselves lost in a fairy black hole." Chaphesmeeso paused for dramatic effect.

"Oooooh," Kenn tried to make a spooky sound, but the effect was closer to an amorous moose.[5]

"Fairies go in and don't come back," said Chaphe. "The changeling remains at large, and the fairies sent to find him are missing. Fairy-whispers now murmur doom. No Changeling has before survived to grow. A goblin-made golem given the power of children, taught

[5] Any rumors about the author and the moose are lies. Vicious lies.

human magic, could very well spell the end of the Make-Believe."

"Doubtlessly," said Clemency.

"So. What's the plan?" Chaphesmeeso grinned rakishly. "Clemency always has a plan."

"I've got no idea what you're talking about," Clemency said. "Can we start over?"

Chaphe looked at Kenn, who shrugged. He looked back at Clemency.

"Then from the top. Where . . ."—Chaphesmeeso lifted a sage finger—"do hobgoblins come from?"

"Ooh! Ooh!" Kenn raised his hand and hopped as if he were wearing an electric diaper. Chaphe ignored him.

"Grab ear, girl," he said, leaning forward.

They tunneled plumb down into the globe, Chaphe and then Clem with a Kenn caboose and a wicked blue fairy glowing like a lantern off the end. They tore through dirt, through rock, and down into clay. Fathoms deeper than well-diggers dream, well within the relaxation of gravity's grip, Chaphe did the last thing in the world Clemency expected. He stopped.

They tumbled on one another into a tunnel, pre-dug, larger, whose marbled clay floor was newborn-warm and glowed faintly red from the closeness of the earth's core. There was a smell of salt water, and a dripping, and beneath that, on the edge of Clemency's hearing, phlegmy whispers that rattled and popped like caterpillars frying in butter. The whispering was coming from beyond a curve in the tunnel ahead.

"Where are we?" whispered Clem.

"The ocean's basement—the goblin tunnels beneath the Leviathan graves. Now hold your peace or rest in it; we're spying a glimpse of wicked things."

They were beneath the ocean. Clemency swallowed and felt her ears pop. The air she was breathing seemed suddenly very precious.

Softly they crept around the bend, Chaphesmeeso cupping the Fairy of Long Goodnights inside his hat to smother her glow.

"Clay-baby-making," the wet, whispering words percolated from ahead. As Clemency's eyes accepted the darkness, two figures resolved from the gloom.

"Clay-baby-clay," whispered one, giggling with a voice of rattling, rotten reeds.

They were like the beef-jerky children in Clemency's child-snatching dream. They were skinny and shriveled, cloven-footed and slender-

CLAY BABY-MAKING

fingered, with two ears like goat horns and two like doornails, limp tails hanging from scrawny bottoms. Chaphesmeeso could have looked like the creatures had he spent a century eating nothing but mosquitoes who also happened to be sucking him dry.

"Goblins," Chaphe whispered. "Hob-naughts. Pure wickedness and chaos. Bitter bitty-brained baby-nappers moiling in clay at the proxy they'll swap for the baby they cop."

Drip . . . drip, drip, seawater shimmered across the tunnel's ceiling, falling in odd rhythm to the floor.

"They've almost finished one," said Kenn. "A changeling."

Indeed, lying between the two goblins was the rough shape of a baby, lumped together from clay. It was unfinished mostly, but some details, an ear, the tiny wrinkled fingers of one hand, were uncannily lifelike. The squish of the warm clay underfoot suddenly made Clemency a touch uncomfortable.

They watched as the nearer goblin pulled clay from the floor, shaped it into a crescent, and pressed it as an eyelid onto the clay baby's face.

The other goblin watched, rocking and giggling, clutching some tiny precious thing to his chest in fingers curled like a dead spider's legs.

"Clay baby. Make clay baby," the first goblin said.

"Make clay live. . . ." said the other goblin, opening his hands to reveal a tiny glass jar filled with purple black liquid.

"Leviathan Ink," whispered Chaphesmeeso. Kenn looked yearningly at the tiny jar.

Clemency watched the goblin, who tweezed the jar between withered fingers and pressed it down into the clay baby's belly, burying it there. The other goblin inserted a jagged finger into the dimple and shaped it into the baby's navel.

The two goblins drew back and waited. Seawater dripped against the floor.

The clay baby's newly pressed eyelids twitched, then peeled back, and two small dark eyes shone in the gloom.

Clemency gasped.

The goblins looked up at the sound.

Chaphe grabbed Clem and Kenn and pulled them back from the bend.

"Act like a drip!" he whispered fiercely to Kenn.

Kenn looked at him, bewildered. Clemency looked at Kenn; neither had she any idea what he was supposed to do or what the goblins would do if they caught them.

After several moments, one of the goblins was distracted by his own foot splayed out before him.

"Toe jam," he said, and rubbed a finger along the webbing between his toes.

"Toe jam," refuted the other, gnawing on his own foundation.

"Good work," Chaphe whispered to Kenn. "Nearly thought you were a drip myself. Let's go."

They took a left and tunneled to Istanbul.

On their way to the night nursery, Clemency stubbed her toe on an Ottoman, who apologized and doffed his fez.

"There!" Chaphe whispered, pointing to a shadow that pulled away from the nursery wall, a goblin with a clay changeling baby under his arm.

Chaphe, Clem, and Kenn watched through the window, eyes just peeking over the sill. The Fairy of Long Goodnights buzzed impatiently behind them, killing fireflies who mistook her wand for an affectionate friend.

The goblin's fingers wiggled gleefully for a moment over the sleeping baby girl before snatching her deftly from her cradle and laying the cunning clay replica in her place.

"That's horrible!" Clemency whispered.

"You should see where human babies come from," Chaphe said.

"We have to stop him!" Clemency said.

"But that's a hobgoblin in the making," said Kenn.

"They're made of clay?" Clemency asked, poking Chaphesmeeso, who felt more like an amphibious pumpkin.

"No, no, no. The changelings are clay, just decoys. Hobgoblins are made of the cradle-snatched babies taken underground by goblins," said Chaphe. "Then we rob the robbers, and get punished for our good deeds by having to raise the little nudnicks."

"Like me," Kenn said.

The clay-baby changeling stretched and yawned in its crib as the goblin shrank back toward the shadows. Holding the sleeping baby so gently in its arms that she never woke, the goblin slipped into the closet, lifted some loose floorboards, and dropped down underground.

The changeling curled up in the crib, and for all the world the nursery looked as if nothing had happened.

"What happens to the changeling?" Clemency asked.

They tunneled to the south of France.

They sprouted from the earth in a tiny town on the coast, next to a Dumpster behind a pastry shop. Chaphe opened it up, and he and Kenn dived into the pool of yesterday's pastries and swam around with their mouths open.

"What does this have to do with where changelings go?" Clemency asked.

"What?" Chaphe said. "We're in France."

They ate day-old almond croissants and walked to the edge of town, which was nearly empty in the first peach-colored minutes of dawn. Kenn tried to feed some almond paste to the boxer tails in his backpack, but their mouths were closed to all but root beer.

"*Bonjour!*" said a nun on a bicycle.

"*Bonjour!*" said Clemency, which she had learned from a book.

They crept through an overflowing vegetable patch surrounding a tall, proud house. Clemency could hear water splashing into a basin, and a woman's voice singing in French. Her words sounded like cursive writing looked. Clem didn't recognize the song but knew immediately the lilting sweetness and loving play of its tone, unmistakably a mother singing to her child.

"I wonder what she's singing about," Clemency softly said.

"Ripping the feathers off a bird," Chaphe replied.

The two hobgoblins, the girl, and the increasingly impatient fairy watched from behind the bottom half of a door that opened like a scandalous bathing suit, in two pieces. This being France, the top was open.

The woman in the blue-tiled kitchen was as young and plump and pleasant as newly risen bread. Her song ended and she began to hum jazzy variations on its tune, bobbing and swaying in time with the music as she sidestepped two ankle-biters on the kitchen floor, one a toddler and one a crawler.

She lifted her third child, a softly cooing

baby boy, from his blankets and carried him toward the white enamel sink. She failed to notice the slight smear of flesh-colored clay left on the blankets. She nuzzled her nose into the baby's pudgy little stomach and then lowered him gently into the sink.

"Here, gander higher," Chaphe said, cupping his hands into a stirrup. Clemency stepped up and climbed the bougainvillea. From her vantage, she could see the baby in his bathwater. The tap was running, water puddling around the animated clay dumpling, then spiraling down the drain. The mother sprinkled a handful of water over the child.

The toddler on the floor had decided to play a game of "marching band" with the crawler, who, upon discovering that he was to take the part of a drum, began loudly to wail.

The mother turned from the sink and scooped the toddler from the floor, tutting him cheerfully and depositing him in a high chair.

As soon as her back was turned, the water swirling into the drain took on a flesh-colored tint. The baby subtly began to spread and diminish, melting like a pat of butter on a hot griddle.

It was all Clemency could do to hold the

scream in her throat. She watched the "baby," who, wriggling and cooing still, diminished and melted into a baby-stuff milk shake. There was a glint in the flesh-colored slurry, a tiny glass jar filled with some deep purple, almost black, liquid. It looked like a pinky-size pot of ink. It swirled down the drain and gurgled away in the thick, watery clay.

By the time the mother had turned again to the sink, the water was running clear.

Clemency dropped from the bougainvillea before she would have to see the expression on the mother's face.

"That's awful," she whispered. "Take me away from here."

They tunneled away but not so fast that Clemency could not hear the mother's scream diminishing behind her.

Two hobgoblins, the girl, and the fairy traveled deeper than the earth is wide and came to a place countless children had entered, but none before had left still a child.

CHAPTER 13

GILBERT MESS LOCKED behind him the door to his father's room and crept to the bedside chest of drawers. He had to be very careful, not for his father's sake, who'd have scarcely noticed a pair of Japanese fighting fish in his beer, but for his brother Inky's, who watched the world as intently as if it would bite him the moment he looked away. It made Gilbert want to bite him.

Mr. Mess would be gone, peddling pickles for several more hours. When he did return, he would be lost for the evening to a beer, the newspaper, and his own vinegar stink. The Mess men were a family of rare bathers and cultivated a rare funk because of it.

As with cheeses, the odor was stronger among the elder than the young, and Gilbert wrinkled his nose as he pushed his father's undershirts gently aside and uncovered the pictures below. Gil imagined Inky standing on the far side of the door, wondering at him. He spread the pictures out on his dad's unmade bed and studied them intently, as he had done weekly since their discovery.

There was a danger in the photos, like the giddy thrill at the temptation to jump when looking over the deadly void of a cliff's edge.

"Mom." He mouthed the word, barely more than a whisper, in case Inky was listening at the door. The word carbonated his blood. Gil could not remember the face of the woman in the photographs, even if he could recognize so many of her features when he looked in a mirror.

She had his heavy brow and large hands, and seemed happy in the pictures, standing beside an incredibly young version of Mr. Mess, or holding in her arms a baby that Gilbert had to assume was himself.

He could remember his dad removing all of her photos from the walls after his mom was taken away. It seemed strange that he could remember that, and not her.

Gilbert wondered again whether Inky had found the photographs as well. He had recently been asking about their mother more and more.

"You were adopted," Gil would answer. "Your mom was a giraffe."

Inky was embarrassed enough by the birthmarks on his face that such a joke would usually silence him. But their vanished mom had become for Inky a sore tooth that he could not stop wiggling.

"What happened to our mom?" Inky would ask.

"Your mom's a blotter."

"What happened to our mom?"

"Your mom's a pair of bloomers."

But no matter how many spotted, stained, or polka-dotted things Gilbert could name (seventeen, try it!) Inky could not be embarrassed out of his fierce curiosity.

"If you ask about our mom again"—Gilbert raised a threatening fist— "I'll conk your noggin."

"Where's our *ouch!*" Inky said. "Where's our *ouch!* Where's our *ouch!*"

Inky cradled his thoroughly conked noggin, looked at the floor, and did not cry.

Gilbert eventually wrote Inky the note that explained everything; it told where their mother had gone and why Inky, especially, would not be able to see her ever again.

It was like throwing a plastic ham to a hungry dog; Gil knew that whatever kept his little brother from reading was more impassable than age, and Inky was too secretive to ask anybody to read it to him.

Gilbert was nearly certain that the note would be lost or fall to pieces long before Inky learned that he had driven their mother insane and driven her away from their home forever.

CHAPTER 14

CLEMENCY WAS BEGINNING to wonder if the world was as shot through with tunnels as a Swiss cheese. She and Kennethurchin had to walk fast to keep up with Chaphesmeeso's purposeful waddling. The Fairy of Long Goodnights threw a faint bluish glow against the walls of the great tunnel they now traversed.

"What exactly is the changeling going to do if we don't find him in time?" Clemency asked.

"He's barreling toward the same barrel he's bent on bending over." Chaphe nodded toward Kenn. "He'll grow up."

"What'll happen then?" Clemency asked.

"Kenn will go bananas and split," said Chaphe. "But his changeling . . . Nobody knows; no changeling has ever grown up before. The fairies say it'll be cataclysmic."

"And how do the fairies know?"

"Fairies know everything. They're dumb as putty, but they know everything." Chaphe hurried onward.

While Clemency was trying to figure that one out, Kennethurchin began to pluck at her elbow. They slackened their pace until Chaphe and the deadly little fairy were out of earshot.

"Clemency, hey Clemency," Kenn whispered, "you know what I worry about?"

"Nope."

"I worry about my changeling. I mean, I know he's not really *my* changeling, but still . . ."

"What's your worry?" Clem asked.

"That fairy"—he nodded at the blue glow turning the bend ahead beside Chaphe— "she looks about as ice as a nice pick. It's her business to, you know . . . kick other creatures' buckets. And she's going to do her business on my changeling."

"That's the whole point of our quest, isn't it?" said Clem. "If we don't find him, you'll go crazy and all the Make-Believe could go kaput."

"Well, yeah."

"And your changeling is just clay."

"Sure. But you and I are just bones and skin and guts. And I guess I've got some ants in me because I found this ice-cream sandwich on the ground that I wanted to eat and tried to brush them off, but they're really kind of sticky little . . ."

"Kenn. Focus," said Clemency.

"Oh. Yeah. So, he's just clay and all, but maybe if he's been alive for nine years, he might have gotten kind of attached to living. I know I would. Or have."

Clemency had never stopped to think about the changeling. What if they found it, or . . . found *him* and he did not want a visit from the Fairy of Long Goodnights.

The selfsame sprite was suddenly hovering a few inches from Clemency's nose, her narrowed eyes the suspicious blue of poisonous toads.

"Oh, hello," said Clemency. She and Kennethurchin grinned like monkeys caught cheating at pinochle.

"Don't hurry on my account, I only get younger and prettier." Chaphesmeeso was waiting by a small doorway dug into the tunnel wall, tapping a metal-tipped toe. He pointed at Kennethurchin. "But you, my half-baked loaf, are running out of time."

Chaphesmeeso stooped and walked through the door, Kennethurchin sheepishly following.

Clemency thought of the homeless lunatic in New York, whom Chaphe had called a "not-gob." He must have been a child raised entirely in the Make-Believe, then denied graduation to goblinhood and dropped so suddenly into adult reality that he cracked.

Was that the fate awaiting Kenn? Clemency thought of how everything messy, eccentric, and charming about Kennethurchin could so easily become filthy, lunatic, and terrifying. It hurt her heart to think on it.

She nearly had to crawl to fit through the doorway behind Chaphesmeeso, but the chamber on the farside could have accommodated a game of elephant polo.

It was enormous, and enormously empty. Clemency could not see the ceiling and could only vaguely guess at the distance to the far wall, her only point of reference being a small table and chair in the center of the room that reminded her of the simple furniture at the library.

A dozen bookshelves had been carved into one wall. There was ample space for thousands of books, but only one tombstone-size tome rested in the center of the entire case. The book had a flickering glow to it, as if a candle burned somewhere inside its thick leather binding.

"You're a long way from hobgoblin-hood, girl," said a voice as musical and gravelly as a concrete clarinet.

Clemency turned to face the oldest living thing she had ever seen. The hobgoblin looked like an argument between a walrus and a pig, stretched over a question-mark frame. Sprays of white whiskers sprouted from his cheeks, on either side of a nose blossomed and mottled like a great pink cauliflower. He wore no hat, and the skin of his bald head was as gray and wrinkled as a smiling mole. Neatly pressed pants covered his hog haunches, and surprisingly delicate hands fidgeted below shirtsleeves rolled to the elbow. In the fob pocket of his banker's vest was a slender pen, made of the same bone-white stuff as the sealed ink pot hanging from a chain around his neck.

"Allow me to present the Tallygob, keeper of the Forgetting Book. He's not so young as he looks," said Chaphe. "And this deceptively small package is Clemency Pogue."

"It's very nice to meet you," Clemency said, extending her hand.

"Hello, Clemency Pogue," said the Tallygob, taking Clem's fingers for a moment in a gentle grip. Then his pinkish eyes found Kennethurchin and the Fairy of Long Goodnights. "Poop in a bag and kick it. Why aren't you on your quest?"

"We are. We're questing right now," sputtered Chaphesmeeso, as close to flustered as Clemency had ever seen him. "Kenn. What are you doing? Quest more."

"We couldn't find my changeling on our own, so we talked Clemency into helping us," Kenn tried to explain.

"We think the changeling's masqueraded his moniker. Nary a clay Kenneth Mess to be found above ground," Chaphe said.

"If that were the case, the case would be solved. You'd have retrieved the Leviathan Ink from the heart of the changeling and the Forgetting Book would give him"—the Tallygob pointed at a chagrined Kennethurchin—"a goblin name, and we'd be dorry hunks. But if fairy-whispers are worth their breath, that wickedly shaped changeling is still at large and raring to throw the balance between good and bad far enough into hob-knows-what that we can all kiss our Make-Believe good-bye." He swiveled his grizzled head toward Clemency. "What do you do that helps?"

"Um." Clemency looked at Chaphesmeeso for help. "I've got moxie."

"She's the jack in our box. Wind her up and she'll surprise you," said Chaphe.

"Let's take your story for a walk. Sounds like Clemency needs to see the Forgetting Book." The Tallygob waddled purposefully forward, Clemency and her companions hot on his hooves.

"All right, Moxie, what've you glommed so far?" asked the Tallygob.

Clemency took a breath, then said, "Goblins steal babies, replacing them with clay changelings that fool the mother until they wash away with the bathwater. Then hobgoblins steal the babies away from the goblins and raise them underground, until they're ready to become hobgoblins themselves."

"Or goblins if they're bad," said Kenn. "Not that I'd want to be one. I'm just saying."

"But Kenn doesn't have pigs legs or rabbit ears," said Clem.

"Which brings us to the Forgetting Book," said the Tallygob. The Tallygob hoisted the tome, more than half his own size, and lugged it to the small table at the center of the room.

"The Forgetting Book," said the Tallygob, "is a book of infinite pages. Open it."

Clemency reached for the book cautiously, worried that it could burn her, so candlelike was its flickering glow. But its pages were cool and dry against her fingertips as she pushed it open, revealing two facing, empty white pages.

"All of the Make-Believe has been recorded in that book," said the Tallygob.

Clemency flipped to the next page and found it empty. A dozen more were similarly blank. The book's candlelight flicker was brighter through the pages, casting an eerie underglow on the girl and her companions.

"It's empty," said Clemency.

"No. There's more written there than in every human library combined. But a book of infinite length can never be opened to the same page twice. Anything written on one of those pages, once the page is turned, is lost forever."

"But I thought only humans could write," said Clem.

"It's humans who write in that book, and it's the last thing they do as humans. Every child

TALLYGOB AND FORGETTING BOOK

under goblin tutelage writes his farewell to humanity by signing his goblin name in Leviathan Ink."

"So why can't Kenn just sign his name?" Clemency asked.

"His Leviathan Ink is still in the belly of his changeling," said the Tallygob. Clemency thought back to the tunnels beneath the ocean floor where she had watched a goblin press a tiny jar of dark ink into a changeling's belly, giving it life. This tome before her was written entirely in such ink.

"Where did the book come from?"

"The book's history and the signature of its binder are on the first page."

Clemency flipped toward the front of the book and found another blank page. She realized that she was not on the first page and flipped the next left over, revealing another blank page. Of course, there was one more page against the binding, which she flipped over, revealing one more page against the binding.

"I guess an infinite book doesn't have a first page," said Clem.

"Of course it does, it's just an infinite number of pages ahead of . . ." The Tallygob trailed off, listening to some distant thing. " . . . of where you are now."

The Tallygob's and Chaphesmeeso's rabbit ears were leaning as if in a stiff breeze. Clemency looked earward but could hear nothing.

"A fresh baby in the goblin den," said Chaphesmeeso.

"Right then," said the Tallygob, bending double and putting the crown of his head to the floor.

Clemency grabbed hold of his ears by reflex.

"What . . . ," she barely had time to say before she was yanked off her feet and pulled down into the ground behind the mad scrabble of the tunneling Tallygob.

They snaked a spiraling curlicue tunnel in a breathtaking rush, skirting the Earth's molten core, and then upward, stealthily plopping into a tunnel of clay that smelled of salt water.

"Did I say you could tag along?" the Tallygob whispered.

"I didn't have time to ask," Clemency said.

"Hush, and stay close. Misbehavior does not moxie make," said the Tallygob.

They were standing before another large chamber, this one filled like a cave of pirate treasure.

Booty, thought Clemency. But no, it was *booties*. She picked up a small, hand-knit baby shoe. There were hundreds of them piled through the chamber, along with blankets, toys, rattles, and pacifiers, the cast-off bed things of kidnapped babies.

The cry of one such stolen child could now be plainly heard somewhere among the mounds of oddments. But below it murmured a rasping chorus of familiar, scriggling whispers.

"Goblins," Clemency said.

The Tallygob nodded. "Nasty things."

"What do they want with the baby?"

"To raise it as a goblin, teach it wickedness," the Tallygob whispered.

"And if they caught us?" Clemency asked.

"They'd tear us to pieces and feed us to the Leviathans. Stay close." The Tallygob and Clemency ran on tiptoes between drifts of castoffs and dived into a pile of footy-pajamas.

They moved from drift to drift, footy-pajamas to teddy bears, teddy bears to blue blankets, blue blankets to hospital bracelets.

They were creeping closer to the baby's wailing and the goblin-whispers both. The Tallygob's ears rose periscope-like over the pile of hospital bracelets, seeking a goblin-free path to the child.

There was a pile of words before Clemency. The plastic bracelets piled there were the tags that had been fastened to the ankles of hospital-born babies. Each one bore the name of a hospital and a child. MARY DONOVAN, SAMAD GHOBADI, VERNON WILLIAMS; the stolen children all had names their parents had given them, and there were thousands of bracelets piled before her.

"Wait here," said the Tallygob. "If any goblins come, try to look like an unsatisfying snack for a cephalopod."

He dashed off toward the crying baby, leaving Clemency with the bracelets. The names swam before her.

The baby stopped crying.

"Snatched-baby snatcher!" hissed a goblin.

"Napped-baby napper!" hissed another.

The Tallygob crashed through the hospital bracelet hummock and skidded to a stop, a newborn infant wrapped in a pink blanket clutched to his chest.

"We ought to run away," he said.

"Is one of these bracelets Kenn's?" Clemency asked.

Scrawny goblin hooves scrambled toward them.

"Bad time for talking," said Tally. "Here."

He balanced the baby on his hip, reached into the pile of bracelets, fished one out, and handed it to Clemency. The goblin-whispers were drawing closer, individual words burbling from their hissing. "Rip . . . tear . . . Leh-vie-uh-thun."

Clemency and the Tallygob ran, the fast-approaching goblin words prickling at their spines like needles. The Tallygob panted and huffed, falling behind, his stubby pig legs no match for the weight of the baby in his arms.

"Here, let me." Clemency took the child from him, shoving the hospital bracelet in the ample right pocket of her burlap pants. In that brief pause, she saw the approaching goblins in the dim light of the chamber, a jangle of sharp limbs, like scarecrows in a hurricane.

She ran behind the Tallygob, the baby surprisingly heavy and warm in her arms.

"Leh-vie-uh-thun . . . Leh-vie-uh-thun . . ."

The Tallygob crashed into a drift of rattles,

sending them flying cacophonously across the clay. Clemency ran through the hail of plastic, curling around the baby to protect it. A hand gripped her arm, and she felt herself jerked off her feet.

Clemency and the baby fell into a pillow-soft drift of blue baby blankets, instantly buried.

"Shhh." The Tallygob put a finger to his lips as the last rattle of the falling toys settled.

Outside the blankets, they heard goblin hooves scamper through the rattles. Clemency looked down at the baby, who blew a spit bubble at her. The baby had a tiny glass jar of dark purple ink hanging by twine from her neck, the same as Clem had seen wash down the drain in France.

The Tallygob's ears, protruding from the blankets, listened to the goblin hooves recede.

"They've lost us," he whispered.

Clemency took the hospital bracelet from her pocket. It read, KENNETH F. MESS; BATCAVE HOSPITAL; BATCAVE, SOUTH CAROLINA.

CHAPTER 15

"IT's A GIRL," Clemency said as the Tallygob took the pink-swaddled baby from her arms. "I thought hobgoblins were all boys."

"Boys and girls both," Chaphesmeeso said. "Not so much difference between us after a hundred years or so."

Clemency peered at the tiny bottle of midnight purple ink hanging around the baby's neck.

"Is this Leviathan Ink?" she asked.

"The very stuff," said the Tallygob. "Recovered from her changeling's fatal first bath."

Kennethurchin looked longingly at the tiny jar.

"I'll find a tutor for the baby-hob," the Tallygob said. "You all have a quest to attend to."

"Now we're talking turkey, turkeys," said Chaphesmeeso. "And Clemency shall be our guide, if not our method. Where to?"

Chaphesmeeso, Kennethurchin, and the Fairy of Long Goodnights all turned to look at her. Clemency felt the hospital bracelet in her pocket, felt the eyes focused on her, the fairy's merciless blue slits, Kennethurchin's hopelessly innocent orbs.

If they found the changeling, it would look exactly like Kennethurchin, a nine-year-old boy whose discovery would mean his death.

"We are talking turkey, right?" Chaphe asked. "Not just gobbling foul to fool some goblins? Fear less, lead more, fearless leader. Clemency must have a plot. Clemency always has a plot."

She did, and planned to bury Chaphesmeeso in it.

"I'll need time to think."

If Chaphesmeeso's nose wasn't so big, he would have fallen over backward.

Clemency winked at Kenn.

"Time to think? Pondering is for the ponderous! Action is the thing! We're questing!"

"I'll need a day," Clemency said, and winked at Kenn again.

"You're winking at me," Kenn said with a grin, then winked back. Clemency put a hand over her eyes and sighed. Kenn said, "I like winking." He winked at Chaphesmeeso.

CHAPTER 16

CLEMENCY EVENTUALLY EARNED her way free of the two hobgoblins and fairy by sheer inaction. In the woods near her forest home, Chaphesmeeso paced as the Fairy of Long Goodnights buzzed in irritated little circles, as if one of her wings had been lost with her patience.

Every wink and waggled eyebrow Clemency threw at Kennethurchin, he returned like a dim-witted dog with a tennis ball, and Clemency realized she would need to be either more conspicuous or more conniving with her coconspirator. She slipped the box of boxer-dog tails from his knapsack while his back was turned and hid it behind a tree.

"Not a solitary plan in that volatile noggin? Not one scurrilous scheme?" Chaphesmeeso asked. The Fairy of Long Goodnights started killing Chaphe's fleas, and he took the hint. He gave Clemency one final, upside-down, suspicious, and disappointed look from between his knees before the two hobgoblins and fairy dropped into the earth and furiously dug away.

Clemency barely made it halfway to her home before a miniature geyser burped from the earth and a familiar voice said, "Have you seen my boxer-dog tails?"

"Is Chaphe . . . I mean . . . your tutor with you?" Clemency asked.

"No. He said I could dig my own way back 'cause I was slowing him down anyway, and if you didn't have a plan he didn't have the time to . . ."

"Got it, got it," Clemency interrupted, handing Kenn the box of tails and whispering into his ear as he took them, "I know where your changeling is."

Kennethurchin looked up from the scrabbling tails and stared wide-eyed and slack-jawed at Clemency. "You know . . ."

She silenced him with a hand to his mouth, aware of Chaphe's unbelievably sharp ears, from which a world's worth of dirt would not muffle a useful bit of information.

"Can you take us to Batcave, South Carolina?" she whispered. Kenn nodded.

Kenn was not nearly so fast a digger as Chaphe, and it took nearly a half minute to cross the world. Clemency had time to catch fleeting glimpses of the gold veins, goblin tunnels, and dragon-bird fossils they passed. Kenn huffed and puffed for the last half mile upward through solid granite before they burst into dappled afternoon sunlight and a pine-scented breeze.

"It has to be easier to climb a mountain from the outside," Kenn said, shaking the granite dust from his ears.

They stood on a mountain furred with evergreens, overlooking the town of Batcave. Clemency could see the hospital below, a schoolhouse releasing its children, a lazy Main Street.

"We need to find a phone book," Clemency said, wondering how many Mess families could be in town. She looked down the mountain and saw a few nestled clusters of homes scattered through the pine trees.

"Mess Family Picklers!" Clemency cried. It was painted in giant white letters on the side of a distant red barn: MESS FAMILY PICKLERS, THE PICKLE KINGS OF CAROLINA.

"Right! Maybe they'll have a phone book!" Kenn said.

* * *

Kenn was nearly pickled by just the smell of vinegar that filled the barn.

"It's not that bad," Clemency said, looking at the enormous copper barrels. Kenn looked like his face was going to suck itself inside out. The barn had a packed dirt floor and clapboard walls hidden behind massive stacks of glistening jars and burlap sacks of cucumbers.

Kenn took a honey bear out of his back pocket and filled his nostrils.

"Thath's bedduh," he said. Clemency was starting to feel a little queasy herself.

"Why are you carrying a honey bear?" Clemency asked.

"Ebergenthy thupplies," Kenn said, dropping the plastic bear-shaped vessel back into pockets that bulged with taffy, caramels, and suckers.

From the pickle barn, they crossed a field of what looked like landlocked lily pads. *Cucumber vines*, Clemency realized, as Kenn used one of the great leaves as a hanky and they stepped up onto the sagging porch of the Mess family home. It was a small wooden house whose original building materials had nearly been crowded out by the patches and props holding it together. It looked like a club house; it looked like a fort made by boys.

There was no answer to Clemency's knock on the door.

"Nobody's home," she said. She pressed her face to a dusty window through cupped hands and saw Kennethurchin inside, waving. He had opened the door and walked in.

"This is somebody else's house," Clemency reprimanded, stepping inside and quietly shutting the door.

"You said nobody was home," Kenn answered. He rummaged through the kitchen cabinets. "There's not a single sweet thing in this whole kitchen. What do they eat?"

The house was warm and cluttered; it smelled faintly of pickling spices. Clemency kicked an empty beer can, then stepped over scattered crayons and crumpled paper, into a bedroom that reeked of boy.

It smelled a bit like goats and looked like goats had chewed on most of its contents. There were two narrow beds with cowboy and space-opera sheets, great nests of dirty clothes, innumerable precious and unidentifiable gadgets, and walls covered with movie posters and pictures torn from magazines.

The room looked like a moment frozen from a hurricane, with one exception. The space beneath the cowboy-sheeted bed was organized like a Spaniard's stamp collection, with meticulous care. Clemency crouched and, like a goose bride, took a gander.

There were candle stubs and strike-anywhere matches, crayons and crayon-drawn pictures of fairies, empty jars and butterfly nets, a great magnifying glass, all manner of tools, and a roll of duct tape.

Crayon-drawn pictures of fairies. Clemency pulled forth a stack of paper and flipped through it. There were dozens of detailed drawings of fairies, their wings, their wands. It was nearly scientific. Somebody was studying fairies.

Clemency flipped to the last page.

"Great jumping jehoshaphat," she said.

There was a detailed drawing of a fairy's two hands. On the knuckle of each finger was a mark, ten in all. They were like letters just far enough away to be unreadable, each character unidentifiable, blurred and smudged by multiple revisions.

Clemency remembered her own discovery, the name of the Fairy of Frequent and Painful Pointless Antagonism, "Tinkasinge," written across the fairy's knuckles. By that name, Clemency had gained complete control over the sprite, had been able to dictate her life, her death . . .

"Clemency!" Kenn's voice from the kitchen had a quiet panic to it.

She dropped the drawing and ran into the kitchen. Kenn was looking at a photograph stuck by a stickystone to the refrigerator. It showed a father and two sons standing proudly before a freshly painted pickle barn. The father was jovial, bald, and bulbous-nosed. The elder son was a red-haired eleven-year-old giant, with a nearly-vicious grin on his broad, freckled face. The younger son was nearly the spitting image of Kennethurchin. Take away his glasses and the birthmark on his face, and he would have sprayed.

"He looks just like me," Kenn whispered.

"Your changeling," Clemency barely had time to say before the front door banged open and the eleven-year-old redheaded giant burst inside.

CHAPTER 17

INKY WATCHED THE DOOR bang shut behind Gilbert and then walked into the barn. He climbed up onto the catwalks and into the murky corner where the burlap sacks were piled as insulation.

He pulled back the sacks to reveal the lightning bug glow of the fairy-filled jar. Fairy light danced off of the wooden beams and cast Inky's shadow over the shimmering barrels of vinegar below.

The eight fairies in the jar glared at their captor with terrible malice. Each tiny little brain behind burning little eyes plotted deliciously painful revenge.

"Go ahead, hate me," Inky said, tapping on the glass. He had stopped hoping they would grant his wish but still believed they were magic. He just had to keep studying them, figure out how to use them. . . .

Gilbert's eyes bounced back and forth as if he were watching a tennis match between Clemency and Kennethurchin. His eyes finally settled on Kenn.

"Who's she, Inky? I thought you were in the barn. How'd you . . ." Gilbert was thinking so hard that his eyes were nearly hidden under his brow.

"I'm Clemency Pogue," said Clemency, mind spinning, "I'm . . . Inky's girlfriend. Is that supposed to be on fire?"

Gilbert turned where Clemency pointed, and she leaned down to Kennethurchin.

"Your name's Inky," she whispered.

"My name's Kennethurchin," he whispered back, "but that's my not my real name; I'll get my real hobgoblin name when . . ."

"Is what supposed to be on fire? Inky? You don't have a girlfriend." Gilbert took a step toward them.

Clemency's brain knocked against the sides of her skull, trying to glom onto a plan. *Inky,* the boy in the photograph, was the changeling. The boy hanging from this explosion of red hair must be his elder brother, or rather—Kenn's elder brother.

"Inky!" Clemency said, nudging Ken. "You didn't tell me you have a brother! What's your name?"

"I'm Gilbert. You don't live around here, do

you? What's wrong with your pants? Are they made out of potato sacks?"

"I'm Kenneth*oof*!" Clemency added an exclamation point to the end of his sentence with an elbow to his ribs.

"This is Inky," she said.

"I know my brother. Except . . . where are your glasses? Where's your *birthmark*?"

"I think he looks handsomer without them," Clemency said.

"Without his birthmark . . ." Gilbert eyed them suspiciously. Through the window behind him, Clemency saw Inky emerge from the barn, head bowed, deep in thought. He was walking toward the house.

"I have to go!" she cried. Gilbert and Kenn jumped. Clemency added, "I oughta go put out that fire. Thanks for a great time!"

She kissed Kenn lightly on the cheek and ran for the door.

"Great to meet you!" she said to Gilbert, who held out a hand that she ignored, slamming the door behind her.

Out in the yard, Inky looked up at her, shocked. He had Kenn's face exactly, a little thinner, hidden behind a birthmark that looked as if it had splattered onto him from a great height, and thick, heavy glasses.

I just kissed a boy, Clemency thought, and spat into the cucumber patch.

"Hey. Those are my daddy's cucumbers," Inky said.

"He's not your daddy," Clemency said, immediately regretting the harshness of her words. "Quick, this way."

Clemency shoved him back into the pickle barn.

"You were in my house. Who are you?" Inky eyed Clem narrowly.

She eyed him right back. He was shorter than her, but there was a strange nobility to him that disarmed Clemency. His arm did not feel like clay but like real human flesh and bone.

"Who are you?" Inky asked again, pulling himself free of her grip.

"I'm Clemency Pogue."

"What are you doing here? What do you want?"

"It's a complicated story," Clemency said.

"Tell it," said Inky.

So she did.

CHAPTER 18

GILBERT POURED HIMSELF a glass of butter-milk.

"Something's going on," he said.

"Yep," agreed Kenn, staring at Gilbert in wonder. An older brother. He had an older brother.

"Did you hit your head? Did that girl . . . Clementine Pork, or whatever, do something to you?"

"She kissed me on the cheek!" said Kenn.

"Where's your birthmark?" Gilbert rubbed Kenn's face with a rough thumb.

"In the picture," Kenn said, pointing at the photo of Inky on the fridge.

"Ha-ha." Gilbert wasn't laughing. He took a drink of buttermilk, then said, "Something is definitely up."

"Absolutely," said Kenn, and winked at his older brother.

"And if this fairy . . ."

"Long Goodnights," Clemency said.

"Right. If she finds me, she'll kill me?" Inky

kept staring down at his hands or up into the rafters above the pickle barrels. He seemed remarkably calm about the fact that he was a goblin-made, animated lump of clay being hunted to the death by two hobgoblins and a particularly lethal fairy.

Inky was trying not to look toward the jar of fairies, but his eyes kept wandering upward. He had not told this girl about the Make-Believe creatures he had captured, unsure of how they fit into the story.

But everything else fell neatly into place, explained every awkwardness of his existence, even the way he felt spongy after his infrequent showers.

"So what are we gonna do?" Inky said.

"I was hoping meeting you would give me some ideas," Clemency said. "You don't look wicked. You're not planning on destroying the Make-Believe, are you?"

"Not that I know of," Inky said, shaking his head. He thought of the letters he had been able to see but not read on the fairies' knuckles by using the magnifying glass. He thought of the letter his brother had written to explain where their mother had gone.

"I'll make you a deal," Inky said.

Clemency listened.

"I can't read," said Inky. "It's what I've always most wanted and never been able to do. If you teach me to read, I'll meet your hobgoblin friend and the Fairy of Long Goodnights, and take whatever's coming to me."

"Teach you to read?" Clemency asked.

"Teach me to read."

"Easy-peasy," Clemency said. "We've got a deal."

They shook hands.

Inky showed her an irrigation ditch by which they could creep to the house without being seen. Through his bedroom window, they watched Gilbert ignore and insult Kennethurchin by turn.

"Gilbert looks mad," Clemency said.

"He wakes up looking like that," said Inky.

"When do your parents get home?"

"Parent. Dad. Tomorrow morning. I want to be reading by then."

Learn to read in one night? A smile nearly surfaced on Clemency's face but quickly sunk when she saw the deadly serious intent in the changeling's eyes.

She looked through the dirty pane at Kennethurchin. She wondered how long she had before he grew up.

"Come on." Inky straightened his glasses. "It's a long walk to the library, and I've got a lot to learn."

CHAPTER 19

THEY ARRIVED BREATHLESS at the low brick building as the librarian was ushering the last few readers out into dusk.

"I'm sorry, we're about to close," the librarian said.

"Ah, we'll come back tomorrow." Inky sounded disappointed.

"But . . ." Clemency barely got the word out before Inky's finger fell on her lips.

As soon as the librarian's back was turned, he grabbed Clem's wrist and dragged her stealthily back into the stacks.

"We can hide here," Inky whispered, lifting from a rack a newspaper hanging by a dowel. Clemency climbed into the dark, newsprint-scented hovel, and Inky followed, closing the paper door of words behind them.

They crouched in their dim gray hideaway, listening to the jingle of the librarian's keys. Clemency leaned against the wall and closed her eyes. It had been a long day, and in the dim light she suddenly realized how sleepy she was. . . .

"Wake up," Inky hissed.

Clemency leaped to her feet in a fighting stance, knocking the newspaper roof from their fort.

"The library's ours," Inky said, crossing the darkened space and illuminating a solitary green desk lamp at a reading table.

Inky was all business. Clemency barely had time to lower her fists before he had lumbered back to the reading table with a teetering stack of large-print books.

"I'm not dumb," he said.

"I never said you were." Clemency yawned as Inky let the books tumble across the table. Clem cracked her knuckles. "Let's get to it. Ready?"

Clemency opened the topmost book and read, "In the raspberry patch behind his home, William Fardel found a bear cub lost and alone." She pointed at the first letter. "This is an *I* and this is an *N*. Together they spell 'in.'"

Inky squinted at the letters as if they were clowns with guns.

"This is an *I*," Clemency said.

"It's sort of . . . wiggling," Inky said, squinting through his glasses.

"What do you mean wiggling?" Clemency asked.

"Like a worm on a hook," Inky said.

"Try it without your glasses."

Inky took his glasses off and squinted at the *I*.

"That's better," he said. "Now it's very clearly wiggling."

Clemency thought for a moment, then grabbed a pen from the desk. On a sheet of scrap paper she drew a vertical line, then added a horizontal line to the top and the bottom. It looked like this:

I

"See," she said, "I drew a bicycle pump."

"Uh-huh," said Inky. He grabbed another pencil off of the table and began to twirl it through the clever fingers of his left hand.

"Is it wiggling?"

"No, it's a bicycle pump."

"That's the letter *I*!" Clemency said.

Inky's eyes, still focused on the three lines, half crossed, and he nearly fell over backward.

"Okay! Okay! It's not a letter! Wait, I'll draw another bicycle pump!" Clemency sketched another *I* on a sheet of paper. "And now I'll draw a, uh . . . penguin facing left with a spike pinning its tail to the ground."

She drew:

N

"And that's a penguin . . .?" Inky trailed off.

"Facing left with a spike through his tail. The important thing is that it's not wiggling," Clemency said, "right?"

"No wiggling," Inky agreed.

"Okay. So," Clemency said, "bicycle pump plus leftward-facing-spiked-penguin spells 'in.'"

"Arhg!" Inky fell away from the page like it had poked him in the eyes. Clemency realized that she had a long night ahead of her.

Three hours later Clemency's eyelids felt like sandpaper. They still had not made it past "In."

Inky scowled furiously at the page, determined to wrestle the words into obedience.

"Should we take a break?" Clemency asked.

"No. I want to learn," Inky said.

"Don't you get tired?"

"No." Inky did not even look up from the page. He was now twirling pencils in both hands, spinning them expertly back and forth through his fingers. Clemency stretched.

"Chaphe . . ." She caught herself and started over. "My hobgoblin friend said Make-Believe creatures can't read. It would be like a human trying to fly."

"People can fly," Inky said. "That's why they invented airplanes."

"But it's different," Clemency said. "Your eyes just won't see the letters!"

"Sure," Inky snorted sarcastically. "Maybe I should just learn to read with my eyes closed."

Clemency shook her head and watched the two pencils spin like propellers in Inky's hands.

Then her eyes bugged, pushed outward by the idea that had inflated inside her brain.

"You're a genius," she said.

Inky looked up. He was not disagreeing with her.

"You're gonna learn to read with your eyes closed," Clemency said. "Here, close your eyes, give me your hand."

Before he could protest, she yanked up his sweatshirt hood and pulled the strings tight, sealing off his face with cotton scrunched like the lemon-puckered lips of an old woman.

"What hand do you write with?" Clemency asked.

"I draw with my right."

"Great." Clemency grabbed the pencil in Inky's right hand and positioned it for writing. She lowered it to the book before them.

"Okay, this is an *I*." She moved his hand over the *I*, tracing the shape in pencil, then moved on to the *N*. "And this is an *N*, together that spells 'in.'"

"In," Inky said.

Clemency grinned.

"Now, if we add a *K* and a *Y*," she said, leading his hand, drawing in the rest of his name in the book, "we get 'Inky.'"

Inky's mouth, framed by its puckered sweatshirt hood, smiled and whispered, "Inky."

"Let's keep going." Clemency began tracing the rest of the letters in the book, reading slowly as she went, "*T* . . . *H* . . . *E* . . . The . . . *R* . . . *A* . . . *S* . . . *P* . . . *B* . . ."

"*E*!" Inky called out before Clemency could, as he recognized the next letter.

"Right!"

"*R*!" Inky called out. "Another *R*!"

"Then *Y*," said Clemency, "and that spells 'Raspberry' . . ."

Inky's hand moved faster and faster over the

letters, his smile getting wider all the time. He had to be guided through the letter only once before his brain snapped tight onto the knowledge.

His grin was so wide and so radiant that it pushed the sweatshirt hood apart, and Inky found himself staring wide-eyed down at his own hand, carving sense out of the sentences on the point of a pencil.

"*P*," said Clemency.

"*A*! *T*!" cried Inky.

"*C* comes next," said Clemency. "Then . . ."

"*H*!" cried Inky.

"And that spells 'patch,'" Clemency said.

They tore through the book like a blowtorch, and then the next, and the next. Within half an hour, Clemency was only reading him every tenth word, when *PH* made an *F* sound, or when a "tear" dripped down a cheek instead of a "tear" ripping down a page.

An hour later, Clemency sat to the side as Inky traced through page after page, silently murmuring the words to himself too fast to be understood. Clemency could barely see him over the stack of books building between them, every single letter inside thickened by pencil lead.

Inky worked like a machine, the only sounds a steady whisper of scribbling punctuated by the quick rasping of the pencil sharpener.

The thrill of discovery was ebbing, and Clemency felt a pleasant drowsiness creeping in. She saw a ladybug crawling intently across the table and smiled.

"I'm gonna put my head down," she said. "Wake me up if you get stumped by any words, like . . . I don't know . . . 'zymosis.'"

"Z-Y-M-O-S-I-S." Inky rattled the letters off quick as a literary tommy-gun. Clemency drifted into sleep, and dreamed of tentacled behemoths sleeping on the ocean floor.

CHAPTER 20

HIS BRAIN WAS ENGORGED and famished both, drowning in knowledge and thirsty for more. The first glow of dawn was creeping into the library when Inky opened a book and found its words already thickened by his pencil's tracing.

Inky looked up for the first time in hours. Clemency was still snoring softly into her crossed arms. Hundreds of books lay vanquished on the floor, but *thousands* more waited on the shelves. He thrilled at the sheer amount of knowledge, whole oceans of words, entire worlds hidden in plain sight all around him.

He felt the weight of the folded paper in his breast pocket. *The note that Gilbert had given him.*

Inky pulled the piece of paper from his pocket and carefully unfolded it. The letters swam before him as always. He closed his eyes. He thought of the empty space in his memories where his mother was. He took a breath and looked again.

He read the note, from top to bottom, slowly.

His breath grew ragged around the lump in

THE NOTE

his throat. A darkness began to shimmer behind his lower eyelids. Tears as darkly purple as wicked eggplants welled up and streaked down his face. Purple tears splattered onto the paper.

Eleven years earlier, Inky's first tears had stained his cheeks, creating the original "birthmark" across his face. The tears now adding runners down his cheeks would be the last he would ever cry. Inky was all dried up.

He lifted a finger to wipe his eye and paused. A bright red ladybug was crawling across the back of his hand. *That insect,* he thought, *has what I don't—*

"A mother," he said softly. He took the ladybug in his fingers and crushed it.

A vague inkling of vengeance against the entire world, Real and Make-Believe both, began to kindle in his mind. If he could find his way into this underworld of hobgoblins . . . If he could learn how they worked . . . If his human "family" thought he were dead . . .

He dropped the note and stood up from the desk. He started walking toward what he had once thought was his home but now knew was only a house.

CHAPTER 21

CLEMENCY WAS STARTLED awake by silence.

She could not see the table or the floor beneath her for the carpet of opened books spread out everywhere, pages darkened by frantic tracing.

"Inky?" she said. She was very much alone. A sinking feeling began to tug at her gut.

She saw the many-creased note lying on the table where Inky had been sitting. She picked it up, eyeing the black splatter marks curiously.

Clemency rubbed the sleep sand from her eyes and read the note.

DEAR INKY

MOM BROUGHT YOU HOME FROM THE HOSPITAL WHEN YOU WERE BORN AND A FEW DAYS LATER SHE WENT CRAZY. SHE SAID YOU WEREN'T HER BABY. DAD TRIED TO CALM HER DOWN BUT THE CRAZIER SHE GOT. SHE SAID YOU WEREN'T HER BABY AT ALL SHE

*WAS SCARED OF YOU. SHE HAD TO
GO TO THE SHARON RIVER MENTAL
ASYLUM BECAUSE SHE WAS CRAZY
AND MIGHT HURT HERSELF OR
OTHERS. SO THAT'S WHERE MOM
WENT.*

—GILBERT

"That's why you wanted to learn to read," Clemency whispered. It made her heart hurt to think of Inky reading the note.

She recognized the sinking feeling; it was the sensation of a terrible mistake. Clemency stuffed the note into a burlap pocket and ran.

"You think an older brother's something," Inky said. "Wait until you've got a *dad*."

"A dad?" Kenn's mind reeled at the word. They were speaking in hushed tones so as not to wake Gilbert in the next room. "What about a mom?"

Inky's pupils narrowed to pinpoints. Kenn shrank like a thread from a flame. Inky took a breath, and the reptilian malice dissolved so completely from his eyes that Kenn was not sure he had ever seen it.

"Just try it for a few days," Inky said. "If you don't like being a human boy, I'll come back and we can switch again."

"I don't know . . ." Kenn screwed up his face, trying to jump-start his brain. "We were supposed to find you and find the missing fairies . . ."

"Hold still, I need to give you a birthmark." Inky held Kenn's head still by the chin, and began applying dark splotches of paint. "I'll tell you what. Just to show that I'm on your side, I'll tell you where the fairies are."

"That would be great," Kenneth said, flinching slightly from the cold paint on his face. Inky looked into the open, trusting face that was in so many other ways the mirror image of his own. He thought of the murderous rage bubbling up in each of the captured fairies. Their release would almost certainly mean this innocent boy's death.

"In the pickle barn," said Inky, "up in the rafters, under some burlap sacks, there's a jar. . . ."

CHAPTER 22

CLEMENCY'S MIND OUTRAN her feet but still did not get anywhere close to the core of the problem. All she could say for certain was that something very bad was happening, and it was probably her fault.

"Chaphesmeeso," she whispered breathlessly as she ran, "Chaphesmeeso, Chaphesmeeso."

Somewhere in the world, the hobgoblin tipped over and tunneled into the earth, and the Fairy of Long Goodnights took to wing.

Clem sprinted past the ominously red pickle barn and clambered onto the Mess-house porch. The door sprung open on her third knock.

"You!" said Gilbert. "Complacency!"

"Clemency," said Clemency. "Where's Inky?"

"Where's Inky?" Gilbert said.

"I asked first."

"He was gone when I woke up this morning," Gilbert said.

"Drat." Clemency scanned the cucumber patch.

"You're not really Inky's girlfriend, are you?" Gilbert said.

"No. I just met him yesterday." Clemency tried to step into the house, and Gilbert roughly grabbed her shoulder.

"What are you doing here?" he asked suspiciously.

"Trying to save the brother you were born with from the changeling you grew up with and both of them from a wicked fairy," Clemency said.

"I don't believe in fair —*oof*!" Clemency's fist in Gilbert's stomach cut the sentence off before any gossamer-winged wishbringers were talked into a doornail impersonation.

Gilbert seemed busy enough sputtering and groaning, so Clemency stepped around him and into the house.

"Kenn! Inky!" she called out, but the house was empty. On the kitchen table, she saw a tin can filled with dark, purplish paint, a brush lying across the rim.

She poked her head into Gilbert and Inky's room.

"Kenn?"

The shoe box that had been home to the

boxer-dog tails was lying open in the middle of the floor, empty.

Somebody had taken the tails. She bent over to pick up the box, and a foot collided with her burlaped backside. Clemency fell like timber.

"You shouldn't of punched me," Gilbert said as Clemency scrambled back to her feet. She tried to push past him, but he stood firmly in the doorway. "If you weren't a girl, I'd clean your clock."

"If I weren't a girl, I'd have some idea how much this hurt," Clemency said, and kicked him in the bathing suit area.

There was a scream from the pickle barn.

Gilbert curled like a shrimp on the floor. Clemency jumped over him and sprinted for the front door. By the time she was on the porch, Gilbert was already back on his feet with a growl, chasing after her.

"Chaphesmeeso!" Clemency said again as she ran across the cucumber patch. Gilbert stumbled off the porch behind her in an awkward, loping run, face still twisted in pain.

"Help me!" came the cry from the barn as Clemency hit the door and hauled it open.

"Inky!" Gilbert shouted. The boy was walking precariously backward on one of the wooden beams crossing the ceiling three stories above the hard cement floor, flailing at the six furious fairies dive-bombing his head.

After the changeling had left, Kennethurchin had crept into the pickle barn, up the ladder, and into the rafters. The six fairies had been hovering inside the large jar, just as promised.

"I've come to the rescue!" Kenn had proudly whispered, clutching the jar between his knees, and with both hands unscrewing the lid.

There was a principle at work here, an equal and opposite reaction for every action. The jar was unscrewed, and Kenn was quite the opposite.

For each of the six fairies, that birthmarked face behind the thick-rimmed glasses had become the bull's-eye in a game of rage. It was not gratitude that they were pouring out onto their liberator. "Hold on, Inky!" Gilbert ran for the ladder leading up into the rafters.

The Fairy of Motherless Children was orbiting Kenn's head like a bad idea, whispering intolerable cruelties about the boy's orphanhood.

The Fairy of Impossible Itches covered the palms of Kenn's hands and feet with maddening torments, like an army of mosquitoes in wool sweaters. Every time he screamed, she darted between his teeth and added another stripe of torment to the roof of his mouth.

The Fairy of Lost Things Found was scattering a year's worth of misplaced straight pins, jacks, and thumbtacks along the beam. The Fairy of Navel Hygiene conspicuously ignored some month-old belly-button lint.

But all of their fury was unmatched to that of the Papercut Fairy, who dived and slashed at Kenn with her nearly invisible wand, every touch another searing, envelope-edge incision.

Then the cucumber patch exploded.

Clemency spun as Chaphesmeeso emerged from the geyser of falling earth.

"I'm very unhappy with you, Clemency," the hobgoblin said, waddling toward the barn through a shower of raw relish.

Gilbert hauled himself up onto the beam high above the hard floor just as the Papercut Fairy slit an X in Kenn's falsely birthmarked cheek, causing him to step back onto a thumbtack. Screaming, flailing his arms, Kenn tipped off the beam. He reached out to catch himself on a post, but Inky's thick glasses blurred and flattened the world, and his hand closed around empty air. Kenn tumbled over the three-story drop toward the cement floor.

Gilbert dived forward and grabbed Kenn's hand. Inky's glasses fell from Kenn's face, bounced off the edge of a pickle vat, and shattered on the floor.

Chaphesmeeso arrived beside Clemency.

"This looks exciting," he said.

"Hold on!" Gilbert gritted through his teeth as Kenn swung by his arm over the precarious drop.

The Fairy of Impossible Itches and the Papercut Fairy swooped down onto Gilbert, strafing his arm with dozens of tiny, searing slices. Impossible Itches landed on the rim of his ear, and Gilbert suddenly had the sensation of a thousand termites in his head. But he was determined not to let his brother drop.

"That's your brother, your real brother," the Fairy of Lost Things Found pixie-whispered into Gilbert's ear.

Clemency lunged toward the ladder, but Chaphesmeeso grabbed her arm.

"That's the changeling," he said. "You have to let nature take its corpse."

"No," Clemency said, frustrated. "He's . . ."

"He's more wicked than even he knows," Chaphesmeeso said. "Fairy-whispers are often obtuse but never wrong. Long Goodnights is on her way; let her do her job."

"Climb up!" Gilbert growled, shaking his head, trying to dislodge the Fairy of Impossible Itches from his ear.

"I can't!" Kenn cried, his fingers slowly slipping from his brother's grasp.

A dim blue glow suddenly arrived, spilling over Clem and Chaphe. The Fairy of Long Goodnights hovered between them for a split moment, her viperlike eyes zeroing in on the two brothers overhead.

"It's him," Chaphe said. "The changeling."

The fairy's eyes narrowed.

Kenn cried out again as he slipped another fraction of an inch. Clemency twisted away from Chaphe's grasp and looked up as the honey bear, abandoning a doomed vessel, tumbled from Kenn's pocket.

The Fairy of Long Goodnights darted upward.

The honey bear broke against the cement floor and splattered sticky golden realization over Clemency's mind.

"That's not Inky," she said.

"Who's Inky?" asked Chaphe.

Pop, answered Clemency. She had become a bee.

She buzzed upward like a fuzzy little rocket. Her multifaceted eyes showed three dozen wicked, blue fairies land on the shoulders of three dozen Kenns. Delicately, with infinite malice, the fairy reached her wand out toward Kenn's paint-stained cheek.

Clemency lowered her head and rammed the fairy in the chest. Long Goodnights dropped her wand and tumbled backward.

Clemency looked at Kenn, who was gradually slipping from his brother's grasp. Kenn was nearly over one of the pickle vats, but not quite.

Clemency butted Impossible Itches out of her way and buzzed, *Swing him over the vinegar* into Gilbert's ear.

Gilbert grimaced and blew a puff of sour air at Clemency.

He doesn't speak bee, she realized.

Pop, she turned back into a girl.

"Swing him over the vinegar," she said, and began to tumble toward the cement.

A moment before crunching against the rock-hard floor, Clem saw Long Goodnights searching frantically for her dropped wand. Half a moment before crunching against the floor, *pop*, Clemency turned back into a bee.

The Fairy of Lost Things Found handed Long Goodnights her dropped wand.

The Fairy of Navel Hygiene took a look at Chaphe's belly button and nearly fainted.

Clemency darted upward, trying desperately to reach Kenn before Long Goodnights did. This time Long Goodnights was ready for her and slashed at Clemency-Bee with her wand. Clemency feinted backward, the wand barely missing her fuzzy yellow belly.

The fairy was willing to kill her! Clemency had never stung anything before; she thought a fairy might be a good place to start.

Long Goodnights swooped back down toward Kenn, who was now swinging slowly back and forth from his brother's arm, one moment over the vat of vinegar and the next over empty space.

Clemency charged the fairy, reversing in

midflight and aiming her venom-spiked behind at the delicate, blue fiend. Long Goodnights spun, and danced aside at the last moment. Clemency-Bee brushed against fairy wing and sunk her stinger deep into Gilbert's arm.

"Agh!" he shouted, but still refused to drop his brother, who was swinging over the cement floor.

Long Goodnights landed lightly on Kenn's hand, in the knot of fingers that joined the brothers.

Her wand descended.

Clemency-Bee buzzed downward.

Kenn swung over the vat of vinegar.

In the split moment before Long Goodnight's wand would have touched Kenn's fingers, Clemency stung him on the thumb.

Kenn cried out and let go of his brother.

Long Goodnight's wand swept through empty air where his fingers had been. Kenn tumbled with a great splash into the pickles.

The boy sank like a stone.

"Inky!" Gilbert shouted. Without a second thought, he dropped from the beam and dived into the vat of vinegar.

He sank like a stone's brother.

Clemency hovered over the vat as the pickles floating on the vinegar's surface bobbed and settled. Long Goodnights, Lost Things Found, Papercut, Impossible Itches, and Navel Hygiene—all the fairies joined her and waited.

Down in the acidic brine, Gilbert held tight to Kenn. They could not open their eyes, their nostrils burned, and no matter how they kicked and swam, the brothers remained sunken at the bottom of the vat.

Even as his lungs threatened to burst and his brain cried out for oxygen, Kenn had a moment to think, *a brother of my own!*

Clemency realized that they weren't going to come back up.

She buzzed to the ground and *pop* became again a girl.

"What just happened?" Chaphesmeeso asked.

"They're drowning!" Clemency said, running around the pickle vat. There had to be a release valve, something . . .

But the shiny copper vat, squatting on its four support posts, offered nothing. Clemency was faced with her own warped reflection in the vat, the Fairy of Long Goodnights suddenly at her side, smiling, content.

Clemency swatted the fairy away and spun toward Chaphesmeeso.

"Dig to me!" she said.

"I'm already here," he said.

"Dig to me, drad nastit!"

"I do have legs, you know."

"Don't make me use your name," Clemency said. "Ch . . . Ch . . . Ch . . ."

She raised her eyebrows and made a sound like a slow-motion locomotive, the hobgoblin's name threatening to slip from between her teeth at any moment. Chaphe looked up at the six attentive fairies and grimaced.

"Whoa, hey, all right. I dig, I dig." He tipped over and with a great rattling crunch, dropped down into the cement floor.

Clemency was alone with the fairies. She locked eyes with Long Goodnights.

The ground beneath her feet began to rumble.

Clemency leaped aside, and a moment later, the cement blew upward beneath one of the legs holding the great copper vat.

Chaphesmeeso brushed the dirt from his clothes.

"There. What could that possibly have

PICKLED

accomplished?" he asked. He did not notice the pickle vat tipping precariously behind him.

Clemency grabbed him by the ears and yanked him across the floor.

With a groan like a groggy iron giant, the great vat of vinegar fell over and crashed against the floor. Gallons and gallons of brine, hundreds of pickled cucumbers, and two half-pickled boys spilled out onto the cement.

Clemency splashed through the vinegar toward the brothers. Gilbert was already on his hands and knees, sputtering and gagging. Kenn was lying facedown in a bed of pickles, the Fairy of Long Goodnights already hovering above him, wand primed for the murderous touch.

"Stop!" Clemency shouted at the tireless blue assassin. She grabbed Kenn's shoulder and flipped him onto his back, revealing a face washed clean with vinegar.

"Hey," said Chaphesmeeso, "it's Kennethurchin."

Long Goodnights sighed dramatically, her wand dropping disappointedly to her side, where it brushed against her knee, and she fell as dead as a gossamer-winged doorknob.

Clemency did not even notice. She was leaning down over the slightly pickled Kenn, an ear to his mouth.

"He's not breathing," she said.

CHAPTER 23

CLEMENCY HELD CHAPHESMEESO'S ear in one hand and Kennethurchin's ankle in the other. They flew down into the earth as fast as Chaphe's arms could pinwheel, Gilbert Mess and four fairies dwindling behind them at the mouth of the tunnel.

Kenn bounced against the walls of the tunnel like a rag doll. There was a lightness to him, exactly the same weightlessness Clemency had felt in Henry before putting him in the ground.

Clem and Chaphe dragged Kenn across the clay floor toward the tiny door that led to the enormous chamber of the Tallygob.

"Hobgoblins are immortal, right?" Clemency said.

"He's still just a boy. A half hob at best," Chaphe replied.

"We have to try," she said.

"Even if it were possible, we don't have the Leviathan Ink." Chaphe sadly shook his head.

"We have to try."

In the chamber, the Tallygob looked from

Kennethurchin's unmoving form to Clemency, to Chaphesmeeso, and then down at his own grizzled hands.

"I'm truly sorry," he said.

"No," said Clemency.

"I really am. There's nothing I can do."

"We can write his name in the Forgetting Book," Clemency said, eyes shining. "He'll be a hobgoblin and he won't be able to die."

"We could have tried," the Tallygob said, "but we don't have the last drops of his changeling's life blood, the Leviathan Ink he would need to write his name."

The Tallygob warbled before Clemency through her tears. Two quests she had failed at: Henry had died and now Kennethurchin.

"It's not your fault," the Tallygob said. "It's Chaphesmeeso's fault for believing in you."

"She did her best," Chaphesmeeso gruffly murmured, then put a hand on Clemency's shoulder. "You did more than anybody could've . . ." His voice began to fall apart and he turned away. "Should've pureed that frog. . . ."

Clemency balled her fists, jaw set against tears. But even now, she was not certain she would be willing to kill Inky Mess, even if it meant saving Kenn's life. She thought of the note he had left behind in the library, written in crayon and stained with blotches of ink.

A splinter of hope lodged itself in Clemency's brain.

She took Inky's note from the pocket of her burlap pants. The blotches of ink at the bottom of the page looked like deformed octopuses, splattered exactly like tears. She thought of the "birthmarks" on Inky's face, the way they traced down his cheeks. . . .

"I have Leviathan Ink," Clemency said, "from the changeling."

The Tallygob looked up; Chaphesmeeso spun.

"It might be dry, but . . ." Clemency held up the note.

"No drier than Kenn is dead, let's hope," Chaphe said.

"Fetch the Forgetting Book," the Tallygob said, drawing the pen from its chain around his neck.

Clemency and Chaphesmeeso hoisted the enormous tome from its stand and carried it over to where Tally crouched by Kenn's side.

They watched the Tallygob touch the tip of

the bone-white pen to one of the splotches on the page. He lifted the lever on the side of the pen, and the tip sucked the blotch off the page, leaving only a dim shadow of a deformed octopus. He repeated the trick on a second blotch, and a third.

"Let's hope it's enough," he said. He gently pressed the pen into Kenn's limp hand. Clemency laid the Forgetting Book down and opened it to a page roughly halfway to infinity. The Tallygob positioned Kennethurchin's hand so that it rested in the center of the page.

"Look away," the Tallygob said, standing and turning Clemency and Chaphesmeeso away from the mostly dead boy and the infinite book. "A hobgoblin's name is a secret thing; it won't work if we're watching."

Clemency stood, a hobgoblin on either side of her, and listened for the faint scratching of a pen on paper. There was only silence behind them.

She felt Chaphesmeeso's hand at her side and took it in her own. He squeezed her hand, and they waited.

CHAPTER 24

"S K A A R P H U N K L E R" was scratched silently across the page in deep purple ink.

He sat up and looked at the letters, and even as he recognized the name "Skaarphunkler" as his own, found that he could not read it. The letters squirmed on the page before his eyes like waltzing worms.

He closed the Forgetting Book and got up onto his hooves.

"Hooves?" he said.

Clemency, Chaphesmeeso, and the Tallygob turned.

"Kenn!" Clemency shouted, and wrapped him in a hug.

"That's not my name anymore," he replied, "but you can call me that if you like. Blegh. Blegh! My tongue tastes like a pickle. Where's my honey bear?"

Clemency let him go and looked at him. Kennethurchin had become a hobgoblin full. Rabbit ears, pig ears, haunches, hooves, a gourd-skinned belly you could bounce nickels off of, the whole kit and enough of a caboodle to count.

"Welcome to the business," said Chaphesmeeso, "but you're still just a beginner, don't forget it."

"Give a thanks to Clemency," the Tallygob said.

"She unkicked your bucket," said Chaphe.

"I was . . ." Kenn looked at Clemency.

"As a doorknob," Chaphe said.

"Doornail," Clemency corrected him.

"Clemency . . ." Kenn's eyes went all puppy dog, and he hugged her again.

"All right, cut the cute." Chaphe wedged them apart. "You're a hobgoblin now; you've got an image to maintain."

She invited all three of them for a root beer, but the Tallygob refused. Keeping watch of the Forgetting Book was his post, and he could not leave it, even for a root beer.

"But I'll be seeing you," he said to Clemency, looking at the silvery fob chained to his vest, "either real soon or never again."

"What did he mean, 'real soon or never again'?" Clemency asked.

They sat in the shade of the willow tree where they had buried Henry. Kenn had been momentarily glum after Clemency told him about the loss of the boxer-dog tails but was now contentedly threading red licorice whips into his left nostril.

"We're into the dragony bits of the map," Chaphe said. "Nobody can say what the changeling's going to do now that he can read."

"You said Inky was going to destroy the Make-Believe," Clemency said.

"And he may yet. We'll be watching for him, waiting for his next move," Chaphe said.

"He didn't seem wicked," Clemency said.

"There's not a thing so widely smiles as cobra hoods and crocodiles," Chaphe said.

"I didn't mean to . . . ," Clemency said. "I'm sorry."

"Pocket your penance. We'd get bored if everything was easy." Chaphe slurped the last of his root beer and hopped to his feet. "There's work to be done."

Kenn snorted mightily. The rest of the red licorice whip vanished.

"Thanks again, Clem," he said, chewing.

Clemency made to hug him good-bye, and he drew away apologetically.

"Hobgoblins aren't huggers," Kenn said.

Chaphe's cheek twitched toward a grin.

"You may do yet," he said, then turned to Clemency. "Luck."

Side by side, they tipped over, touched the pointy tips of their hats to the grass, and dropped back underground.

Clemency was contemplative as she and her father made dinner. She thought of Inky Mess, the goblins, the Leviathan den, and the Forgetting Book. She was so preoccupied that she almost did not notice the Fairy of Awkward Silences fluttering between her and her dad.

Her mom tumbled home exhausted, and they fell to dinner.

"So what did you do today?" Mrs. Pogue asked.

"Oh, not much," said Clemency.

After hot chocolate and a thorough tooth-brushing, as her dad was tucking her into bed, Mr. Pogue asked, "Are you still mad at me?"

"What for?" Clemency asked.

"For cropping the boxer-dog tails," said Mr. Pogue. "For . . . Henry."

"No!" Clemency said. "No, it's okay, Dad."

Mr. Pogue smiled and kissed her on the forehead.

Later, as she was drifting off to sleep, Clemency heard her father say from the next room, "She was so quiet today."

"She's just growing up," her mother said.

Clemency wondered if growing up meant that she would lose her taste for adventure. Even now, she thought how nice a little boredom might be.

She would not be lucky enough to find out.

EPILOGUE

THE BOXER-DOG TAILS led him to the last tunnel Kennethurchin had dug. Along with the hound-snakes (as Inky had taken to calling them), he had stolen his twin half-hobgoblin's knapsack. The houndsnakes were by now the size of weasels and only barely fit into the bag, which was already stuffed with blank notebooks, a mason jar of yellow pencils, and a small silver sharpener.

He had spied, hours earlier, from the edge of the pine trees, Gilbert trying to explain to their father where he had gone. Inky had smiled to see his brother, usually so smart and confident, reduced to stuttering, halfhearted explanations. It had made Inky feel powerful, a new sensation, and one he liked very much.

Inky shrugged into the knapsack and lowered himself into the tunnel. Reading had opened new worlds to him, underworlds and overworlds, Real and Make-Believe, all of them ripe for conquering.

The End

ROOT BEER